ENCHANTER WITCH ACADEMY

A Paranormal Fantasy Romance

PAIGE STONEBANK

TABLE OF CONTENTS

CHAPTER 1:

WILDFIRE

I watched a single flame dance on my fingertips.

It was small, the size of a thumbnail all around. It flickered and burned without a source. The color danced animatedly, the body burning so bright it was nearly white before fading to yellow, then orange, then red. It sucked the moisture from the air, leaving dryness and heat behind. The flame flickered again, then took a shape.

The flame became a ballerina, no taller than my index finger. Her skirts were made of fire, but then again, so was her entire body. The flames that should have been hair were long, dancing in the air as she twirled, jumping from one finger to the other. It was a game to the ballerina. She jumped, and I had to catch her—if I didn't, she'd fall to the floor of the clearing and set the grass on fire. It was a dangerous game that we were playing, but the ballerina seemed adamant. I could do nothing but play along.

The forest around me seemed to hold its breath, waiting for something to go wrong. It was waiting for me to mess up, to let the ballerina fall. It only took one flame on the grass to burn down the entire forest, and my stomach turned as I watched the dancer intently.

This was fine, though. The flame was still small, still too small for me to lose control over. It was when it grew… when it turned my blood to lava and my skin to hot iron. That was what Headmistress Helena said my skin felt like. Like a cauldron that had been sitting over a fire for too long. After my last burnout, the nurses had blisters on their hands for weeks. I preferred not to think about it. Thinking about it gave it power, like how thinking about uncontrollable flames reminded the fire that it could consume me whenever it wanted. No one else spoke of it, either. They were too afraid, the kids at the academy, too afraid of me to mention my mistakes. I could turn them to ash with a snap of my fingers, after all. I didn't blame them. I would have been afraid of me, too.

The ballerina paused, cupping her ear and leaning to one side, listening. I did the same. Footsteps sounded in the forest that surrounded the clearing. I didn't bother looking for the perp; it was too dark in the forest, anyway. No sun could penetrate through the canopy of leaves, it could hardly peek through the heavy, pregnant clouds overhead.

The air smelled like rain and smoke. But there was another scent, too. A sweet scent. The sort of scent that came with magic. I sniffed again, rolling the taste in my mouth, feeling the magic teasing my own. I didn't have to see to know who it was. They were watching; the academy was always watching. Always afraid that I would lose control. Again, I didn't blame them.

The ballerina raised her eyebrow, her tiny face contorting. She was questioning my decision to ignore the other presence. She grew a little, first reaching the size of my middle finger and then the length of my hand. I scowled at her. These damned flames, with their minds of their own. This was why I couldn't control my magic—these questioning flames that never seemed to listen to or trust me. It was infuriating, but there was nothing I could do about it.

The flame grew hotter, burning my eyes and making it hard to breathe. The ballerina morphed into a ball of fire, no longer the gentle, playful thing it was before. No, this was more dangerous, hotter—the sort of thing that people were afraid of. The sort of thing that I was afraid of. I took a step back, instinctively trying to shake the flame from my finger as it singed me. It burned through the protective layer of magic that was supposed to prevent the blaze from consuming me. The fire didn't seem to get the memo.

The flame fell to the ground and, to my horror, ignited the grass at my feet. A perfect circle of fire erupted around me, burning my boots, my legs, the hem of my skirt. Panic boiled inside of me, tears stinging my face. I tried to call the flames back into myself—rather it consume me than the forest and the creatures within.

Then I was drenched in water, wave after wave washing over me. I could feel the liquid evaporate as it touched my skin, but it kept coming. I gasped for air, falling to my knees. The water—sweet, cold water—found its way into my mouth, filling it up with the taste of magic. I choked on it as it finally penetrated the heat, boiling against my skin. Then, there was no heat anymore. Nothing but the waves that extinguished my flames. My heart pounded in my throat; my ears rang. A headache was forming in my temples. Gods damn it all.

"Didn't the headmistress tell you not to go into the forest?" The voice was distinguishably male. It wasn't rough—it was smooth, like honey.

I opened my eyes to find a pair of shiny black shoes in front of me. I sighed. "Actually, she didn't."

Another wave rolled over me, knocking me over so I was on my back. I looked up at the man smirking down at me from above.

The professor was one of the youngest at the academy. In fact, I was certain he *was* the youngest. He was every girl's dream and every boy's nemesis. His eyes were the color of his waves: blue, with flecks of green and silver. He had a chiseled chin that looked to have been carved from marble, and a barely-there stubble that gave him a rugged, bad boy look. He was a handsome man, but he was also a very gay one.

"Feel like lying to me again, Miss Strange?" He raised an eyebrow at me and I heaved another sigh.

"I don't know where else to practice. I can't do it in the dorm, there's too many people. And the teachers never let me participate in the classes, either. Apart from you, of course, Mr. Henry. How am I supposed to learn how to control my magic when I can't practice?"

I've had this same conversation with the headmistress, who merely told me to be patient. That I would one day have a grip on my magic, and I wouldn't have to be treated with caution anymore.

Mr. Henry shrugged. "Perhaps you should befriend your magic before you try to tame it."

I scowled at him. "Well, I can't do either if no one lets me." I paused for a moment, staring at the grey sky behind him. "Please don't tell anyone."

"I am no snitch, Lia." He smiled. "But I don't like you

endangering yourself and the whole forest. If I wasn't here, things could have gotten very ugly. I could hardly put out the little circle of fire around you, never mind the entire forest. Your magic is too wild to be handled with this little caution."

"I know," I said, sighing again as I took his outstretched hand. A wind blew over us and I shuddered. I didn't dare call on my flames to heat me up. "Thank you for saving me."

"Listen, kiddo, we'll figure something out, okay? You don't have to do this alone. I know you feel like you do, but you don't. The headmistress is the only one who could save the forest if it got worse and I wasn't here to extinguish it first. If you don't want to tell her that you're coming here, at least tell me. Hell, I could meet you here every day after school and we can train for a bit."

It wasn't the first time he had offered to train with me, and every time, I had declined. Why? Because I didn't want help. I didn't want to *need* help. I was the most powerful witch at the academy—surely, I could tame a few flames. But now, now that it had taken me years and I was still nowhere near controlling them, I was starting to see that help wasn't a bad idea at all.

"I would like that," I started, twisting a strand of red hair and watching the water drip from it. "What will we tell the headmistress?"

Mr. Henry raised an eyebrow. "We don't tell her anything. She won't approve, now, would she?"

"I suppose not."

"Now," he said, crossing his arms and looking up at the sky, "it's going to rain soon. That could be a good excuse as to why you are soaked. The only question remains is where you were."

"Maybe I had to take a walk? She said I shouldn't practice magic in the forest, but she didn't say anything about taking a walk."

Mr. Henry grinned. "Perfect. Now, if you will excuse me… I may be a water wizard, but I do hate getting caught in the rain."

I watched him disappear into the forest, my stomach twisting. Not with dread, no; it was something else. Could it have been excitement? Perhaps, but I couldn't tell for sure.

My flames were getting out of hand and I doubted Mr. Henry had offered to help me from the goodness of his heart. No, they were all afraid of me and what I would eventually become. If they could help me control my powers, it was easy enough to control me—if they controlled me, they controlled my fire. Still, there was a flame of excitement in my chest. I wanted to tame my fire. If not to control it, to bury it away deep inside of me. I didn't want it in the first place. But if I could tame my fire, I could bury it. It was as easy as that. Perhaps I'd be able to live a normal life in the city. Or perhaps that was too much to ask for. Still, I could always hope.

I smiled as the cloud tore open above my head. The drops of rain soaked into my skin, turning it to ice. I couldn't feel my fire anymore. I loved water; it was the only thing that kept the flames away.

I stayed there for another minute or two, making sure that I was drenched completely, snuffing out my flame. It felt good to feel the fire go out inside of me—refreshing, safe, and normal. And that was all I ever wanted.

CHAPTER 2:

SPIRIT

"You're wet," a voice said as I entered my room in the tower. At first, I'd been excited to get my own room, far away from the other students. This was until I realized that it wasn't because I was favored. No, it was to protect the other students from me.

The west wing was close to being abandoned, with only four classrooms and a handful of teachers who lived here— teachers who could put out my flames faster than I could ignite them. Still, I enjoyed my own space. Every other student had to share with two other people in a room smaller than the top of the tower. Even if I wasn't a complete social outcast, I would have preferred this. It was quiet and remote, with a killer view of the sunrise.

I shrugged off my blazer, heading into my en-suite to get a towel. "Thank you, captain obvious."

The mirror above my sink rattled as Fiona flew through the wall and the mirror. The transparent ghost hovered next to me, her lips pinched into a smirk. Fiona had the horrible tendency of appearing exactly when I didn't want her to. It was like she sensed it, drawn to it like a moth to a flame. It annoyed the seven hells out of me sometimes — now being one of those times.

"I swear, you're like a pet — staying outside until you're soaked, and then trudging your way inside like you own the damned place." She pointed at the wet trail I had left behind. "You look like a snail."

"Don't you have other dorms to go haunt, Fi?"

Fiona looked disgusted, her white hair floating around her as if she were underwater. "I do not *haunt*, Cornelia Strange, and you know this."

Stripping down to my underwear, I wrapped a towel around my chest, the fabric hot against my icy skin. I shivered. I turned to look at her. She was now lounging in the bathtub, one leg tossed over the side.

"Could have fooled me," I told her. "You seem to torment me every chance you can get."

"Is that really any way to speak to your only friend?"

I rolled my eyes. "I do have friends, you know."

"But are any of them as good-looking as I am?"

"Never," I assured her, chuckling.

I made my way back into the room, where I rummaged through my closet. There weren't many options. Most of my belongings came from the headmistress herself, so whatever I didn't get myself consisted of only uniforms and blazers. "No one can pull off the deathly glow you have going on."

"I thought as much." She grinned as her head popped through the wall of my dresser, examining every item I pulled out and held at arm's length. "By the gods, honey. You should have gotten rid of that shirt years ago."

I scrunched up my face, examining the shirt in my hand. It was the first band T-shirt I'd ever bought. It was a local band, and the backup vocalist had hand-painted every piece of merch they sold. It felt too personal to get rid of, even if it did have more tears than I cared to admit. I pulled it over my head regardless of what Fi thought. She was a 50-year-old ghost—what did she know about style, anyway? *Enough to know that torn band T-shirts haven't been a thing since the early 2000s,* the back of my mind told me, but I chose, like I usually did, to ignore it.

Fiona pulled a face. "It's a good thing you're so pretty, because that's the only thing going for you at this point."

"Thanks?" I turned to the mirror on the inside of the wardrobe, the towel now around my hips. I looked into my own eyes, trying to find a sense of normality in them. I couldn't find it in the gold around my pupils, nor the green it faded into, not even in the blue that surrounded it all, keeping the wealth of colors away from the white of the rest of my eyes.

I couldn't find it in the red of my hair, either. It was the color of my flames: oranges, reds and yellows. I thought it was a good idea to spruce up my natural dark ginger hair with yellows and dark reds. It was a spur of the moment thing last summer, and I had regretted it ever since. More than once, I'd considered taking a pair of scissors to it, but Fiona had stopped me every time. She said it gave me character; it made up for my lack of personality, apparently. My skin was a whiter shade of pale, a stark contrast against my red hair and dark brows.

"You gonna wear pants, or are you just going to the dining room with that towel wrapped around your hips?" Fiona was now speaking from across the room, where she had draped herself over my bed as if she owned the place. I sighed.

"Mr. Henry offered to help me with my magic," I confessed, completely off-topic as I searched for a pair of jeans that actually fit. Those second helpings of dessert I've been indulging in were taking a toll on my hips. I found a pair, then turned around to show it to her and she shook her head. I turned around to locate another pair.

"And did you accept this time or shoot him down again?"

"I accepted." I held up different pants and she shook her head again. I was running out of options.

"You did? What made you change your mind?"

Had Fiona owned a physical body, I would have heard her rustling on the bed so she could perch on the end, listing intently. I settled on the first pair of jeans I'd held up for her and pulled them on. I wasn't about to spend my entire evening letting Fiona decide on my outfit.

"Lately," I said, refusing to look at my hands, to acknowledge the magic tingling beneath my skin. It felt like thousands of ants crawling beneath my skin, pinching and biting as they went. It wasn't unpleasant, though, even if I did want to say otherwise. It was merely uncomfortable—but the sort of discomfort that drove people mad, in time. "The fire has been…"

"Hotter?" she asked, completing my sentence.

I nodded. "It scared me today. I was out in the forest, trying to get a hold of the magic, but it got out of hand."

Fiona's face softened, and I knew what she was thinking.

I reminded her of herself. Thirty-two years ago, she was 18, just like me. Her fire magic had consumed her and caused her inevitable death. Perhaps she was only around to keep an eye on me, to guide me. I didn't know why her soul was still here. There have been plenty of other deaths in the academy, and no other ghosts were left behind. None but Fiona. Was it her magic that kept her here, or was it something else? Was it her determination to prevent what happened to her from happening to anyone else? Was it her catty personality that had gotten her tossed out of the afterlife? No one really knew.

"I remember that feeling as if it was yesterday," she said, staring into the distance. I could have sworn her transparent white form burned a little hotter. "I let it go too far. I'm glad you're getting help."

"Do you really think it'll work? Do you think I can control it?"

"The thing with fire is that it's impossible to control. You can't truly control an open flame. Every time a bonfire is lit, the risk is there that it'll get out of hand. One spark, one idiot who just steps too close to it… it's like a forest fire. Even when you think you've got it under control, it's still just beneath the surface, simmering." I shuddered, but she didn't seem to notice. She was lost in thought, lost in the memory of what the magic felt like. "Unless every single part of it is extinguished, there will always be a risk of the flame reigniting."

"You didn't answer my question," I said as I grabbed a pair of Converse sneakers and sat down next to her.

Fiona got up and shrugged. "I think it's worth trying. I think afterwards, the regret of not seeking help is worse than regretting what you did. I know that's the case with me. I regret not letting anyone know just how dangerous my flames were getting."

"What exactly happened to you, Fi?"

Fiona looked at the door, then back at me. "That's a story for another day, Lia. I promise I'll tell you one day."

I didn't push her any further. Her promise was enough for me. Still, I itched to know. I had to know what happened to her so I could somehow prevent it happening to me. I've seen the scars on her legs, the burnt tissue that didn't disappear after death. Sometimes, her dress lifted up just enough for me to get a glimpse of it. But I only ever had a second, because she was very keen on hiding it. I knew she'd burned herself to death, but I had to know how. I had to know what had triggered her, what her magic had felt like before getting out of hand. That way, I would know what to look out for. That way, I could find a solution before it happened.

Soon, she'd tell me soon. She promised.

"I wonder what's for dinner," I thought out loud.

Fiona turned to grimace at me. "How can you be so excited for this food? They haven't updated their recipes in 32 years."

"If it ain't broken, why try to fix it?"

"Easy for you to say." Fiona rolled her eyes. "You grew up with this crap. You don't know anything better."

"Exactly, so don't ruin the best part of the day for me."

Fi rolled her eyes, smiling at me with a mischievous look in her eyes. The little minx already knew, no doubt having spied on the cooks. "It's mac and cheese."

CHAPTER 3:

HALF-TRUTHS

The west wing was far less modern than the rest of the academy. At first glance, one would think that they were two different buildings, owned by two very different people. The west wing still had stone walls lined with sconces. The windows were stained and in those rare occasions when it wasn't cloudy, the sun peeked through them, sending the colors of the windows across the marble floor and walls—faded greens, yellows, and blues, and perhaps some reds and oranges here and there.

But that was not the case most of the time, and it left the halls feeling barren and empty. It was as if there were hidden phantoms in the cracks of the stone. Age had not taken away from the beauty in those windows. They were all scenes from a distant past. The headmistress told me that the windows represented the founders of the academy, and as each of them died, their faces were added to the windows. Each window told the story of the life of that founder, once upon a time. But age and neglect had faded the windows, and multiple pieces had to be replaced. Now there were holes in the pasts of these founders, histories that we would never know. Their stories would never be seen by the residents of the west wing ever again. It was heartbreaking. If I died, I wanted people to remember me. I didn't want my story half told.

There was a howling somewhere in the distance. I knew better than to expect ghosts. Fiona had nearly bitten off my head when I'd asked her whether or not the moaning was from other ghosts. Apparently, it was "insensitive and stereotypical" of me to ask. The wind, that was the real cause of it. There were cracks in the stones that let air in, and it whistled and howled as it blew through. It made the west wing a permanent freezer. I didn't mind; I loved the cold.

I pulled my jacket tighter around me, trying to block out the chill that tried to seep into my bones. It was going to be rough sleeping tonight. There was no heating in the west wing, and I didn't want to risk lighting a fire in my tower. Fires made me uneasy, especially when I was left alone with them. No, I'd rather wrap myself in blankets like a sushi roll than risk my magic getting out of control while I slept. No fires big enough to have an impact on the cold, anyway. The sconces were fine. Their flames were small enough for me to ignore. They were small enough that I couldn't focus my magic on lighting them; instead, I needed matches to do so. That was the way I liked my fire—not caused by me.

I took a left turn, my shoes squeaking on the marble. The sconces weren't lit yet and there were no windows that allowed in the little light from the cloudy sky. It was gray in the hallway, and it took all of my self-control not to start running. I knew that if I did, I would be making more noise than I already was. I had to remind myself that there was nothing to run from, nothing but emptiness. Still, my mind wouldn't give it a rest and I found myself picking up the pace, certain that I felt someone's eyes on the back of my head. Perhaps it was just the emptiness of the hallway waving me goodbye, telling me that it would see me again very soon.

***

In the dining hall, groups of students were huddled together, discussing the day's events and what each teacher had done that day. It was hard to ignore the silence that fell over the hall when I entered. It always seemed to happen. As soon as I entered a room, the cheerful chatter became hushed whispers. I knew those whispers were about me, but I chose not to listen too closely.

I knew how it went by now. They were afraid of me exploding, afraid that I might turn someone to ash. Idiots, all of them. As if the headmistress would have allowed me to sit in the dining hall with the other students if I were that dangerous. They had enough power in this room to put out my fire before it had time to reach the person next to me and they were all watching, ready to suffocate my magic.

The dining hall was an average cafeteria with a fancy name. There were no big oak tables or feasts laid out on them. There were no floating candles or magical violins that played music without a musician. No, everything aside from the west wing was pretty normal looking. If you didn't know it was a school for sorcerers and sorceresses, you would never have been able to guess by looking at the interior. The teachers sat in their own dining hall, only a handful of teachers rotating through the students' hall to keep the peace. Mr. Henry was on duty tonight, sitting at a table with four other teachers. He was chatting with them, laughing animatedly when someone made a joke. I pulled my eyes away from him. Our practicing together was supposed to be a secret.

I cut the line to get my mac and cheese. Who was going to stop me? Everyone was too afraid, too chicken to confront me. I could do what I wanted. That was one upside of being the most feared kid in school. No one had the guts to do anything about it.

I didn't have to look for my usual crowd. They were seated at their usual table, speaking loudly over the hushed voices of the rest of the hall. I grinned. They never seemed to disappoint. There was always a point to be made, a wound that needed salt, and they weren't afraid to be the ones who handed it out. My usual seat was unoccupied, and I took it without a second thought. I smiled at them.

"Is it just me or am I getting more popular?" I asked, piling as much food on my fork as I possibly could before stuffing it into my mouth. It wasn't nearly as creamy as I remembered my mother making it, and it didn't have the same amount of cheese, either. Still, it tasted magnificent on an empty stomach.

"Quite the opposite," Wendy said, picking at her macaroni as if it was offensive. "They heard about you in the forest this afternoon."

I froze mid-chew. "How?"

Instinctively, I glared at Mr. Henry, who was looking straight at me. He shook his head and went back to his conversation with Ms. Evergreen. Of course, it wasn't him. He wasn't the sort of person to occupy his time with boarding school gossip.

"Margot said she saw you talking to a demon made of flame. She said he was as big as your head," Damien said from next to me, his brown eyes dancing with amusement. I glared at him.

"It wasn't a demon," I corrected, finishing my bite before taking another. "It was a ballerina."

Patrick burst out laughing, the entire hall's faces on him. He waved a hand at them dismissively. "As you were, peasants." He turned back toward me. "A ballerina?"

Patrick was the sort of guy that didn't entertain idle gossip. He was a man of the people, with dreadlocks that reached his waist and piercing golden eyes that had me briefly convinced he was wearing contact lenses. I then realized that we were all only 14-year-olds, and I didn't think he even knew about contact lenses back then. He'd come from a tribal coven in Africa, and when his parents moved to America, he was forced to leave his humble beginnings at home. The poor guy spoke only the most basic English and had worn a robe for two whole years before trying jeans for the first time.

But he was the sort of guy that everyone wanted to be friends with. Perhaps it was because he didn't gossip, or he shut it down before it could even begin. He said that gossip was the devil's most entertaining activity, and he wasn't going to have any part of it. Needless to say, there were never any scandals surrounding him, and he was a refreshing addition to our group. I still didn't understand why he sat at the loner table, but I supposed his foreign heritage made him somewhat of an outcast, even though he hardly even had a noticeable accent anymore.

"I like ballet, sue me." I shrugged. "And we weren't talking, we were playing catch."

Wendy rolled her black-lined eyes. Her makeup was as caked on as ever but somehow, she made it look good. I'd asked her to do the same look on me once, but she had refused, saying that my hair was far too loud and it would distract from my makeup. I didn't argue with her. "I don't know how you manage to do this every time."

"It's not as if she does it on purpose, Wen," Pat growled at her, then winked at me. It was his way of saying "no problem," even though I hadn't thanked him. "If she was doing it on purpose, she would have made a public show of it," he continued, playing with the ring on his middle finger, which was engraved with a tree of life. We'd tried to ask him what it's all about, but he'd refused to tell us, saying it was a mystery. I was certain it was just a random ring that he'd picked up at the dollar store.

Nina elbowed me in the ribs. "Don't look so sad, Blaze." The macaroni went sour in my mouth when I heard the nickname. "At least you're never as invisible as the rest of us."

"You're saying that as if it's a good thing," I said, swallowing hard before taking my next bite. My plate was nearly empty and I was still starving. "I'd love to just fade into the shadows."

"I'd hate to see that day." Damien smiled at me and, instinctively, I smiled back.

Wendy gagged.

"I'm just saying," I said with a shrug, the silence making me uncomfortable, "it wouldn't be a bad thing to just be able to disappear."

"Perhaps you shouldn't care so much about what you can't change and focus a little on what you have." The table went silent again after Wendy spoke. She knew better than anyone that there was no way to change yourself, no matter how hard you tried. Wendy's magic involved transformation. She could change any inanimate object into something else for a short period of time. She could alter the appearance of almost everything, except one thing: herself.

Looking at Wendy, with her short black hair, her piercing blue eyes, her porcelain skin, and the black makeup around her eyes that sometimes made her look like a skeleton, one wouldn't think there was a self-conscious bone in her body. But it hadn't taken the four of us long to realize that Wendy was just as messed up as we were.

She, too, wanted to be normal. It must have been hard, being able to change everything except the one thing she wanted to. It must have been hard, watching everything else change shape and color while she stayed the same. It was easy to forget that Wendy had a heart, after all. She didn't seem like the sort of person who had an abundance of feelings. She was always cold, always rude. But we all knew it was a coping mechanism. She needed one of those when she went back home for the holidays. I didn't think anyone would want to spend their holidays at the academy instead of home. Wendy was the one exception.

She pushed her plate of food away from her body. She always did this, took a few bites, then shoved the plate away. Her dinner was up for grabs. I didn't need to be told twice. I pulled the plate closer to me.

"It tastes like cardboard," Wendy complained, changing the subject.

"Food is food," I replied, taking a bite of the macaroni.

Now that she mentioned it, I could taste the cardboard. It didn't bother me, though. I was still starving, and I wasn't one to turn down any form of food. Not even when it tasted like pan-fried cardboard.

Except when Cook Dolores was on duty. Then, we got steamed vegetables and meat that didn't taste, look, or smell like meat. The mystery meat was still okay if you closed your eyes and pinched your nose, but the veggies were awful. She was particularly fond of zucchini… and I hated zucchini with a burning passion. I was certain Dolores only served it because she knew the students hated it.

But thank the gods that it was Cook Magda on duty tonight, which meant we got creamy cardboard and a whole lot of carbs.

CHAPTER 4:

SWEET DREAMS

I was being devoured by flames. They were large and hot, scorching my skin and making my eyes tear up. The heat was unbearable, and I was sweating. I couldn't see where I was, couldn't see where the flames started and where they ended. The iron I was standing on was heating up, turning red with heat as it started to burn through the soles of my boots.

The flames licked at my face, my hands. I tried to manipulate it, but it was no use. These flames were wilder than mountain lions. They were hungry, as if they hadn't eaten in weeks. They prodded at my skin, flicked at my hair like children teasing the weird kid in class. I could have sworn that they were singing. The tune was vaguely familiar, but nothing I could put my finger on. It was impossible to hear coherent words through the crackling of the blaze, through my panic and fear.

I fell to my knees, my head in my hands. The song grew louder, louder… It was a lullaby, one that I'd heard a very, very long time ago. Or was it? The words didn't make sense. Were they in a different language? It sounded Latin, but where would I have heard a Latin lullaby? I was losing my mind. I was losing my sense of self. That was the only explanation, the only thing I could think of that made sense. Then again, nothing made sense anymore. I was cocooned in fire that I was not able to control. I was being eaten by a beast that had no physical form.

I always knew this was how I was going to die; consumed by the very thing that I was supposed to control. Control… I huffed, wiping the tears from my cheeks as the hot iron below me began burning through my jeans. I didn't flinch. If my flesh charred, it would have been easier to endure. I would have had an armor against the flames—an armor of burned flesh was better than no armor at all. It was the one thing I could control in a world that I should have been able to control. I chuckled bitterly. What was control, anyway? I wasn't even sure I knew what that word meant. There was no controlling the flames. It didn't matter how hard I tried, or how I avoided them. They were going to consume me one way or another—either angry because I'd neglected them, or angry because I'd tried to control them. There was no winning… All I had to do was accept it. And I controlled what I accepted. Yes, that much control, I did have. I chose to accept it and I chose to make peace with my death.

I had to expect my inevitable demise, burned to a crisp. It was a horrible way to go. It wasn't at all like the death I had imagined as a child; heroic and sacrificial. Yes, I'd dreamed of being the hero, of giving my life to save the people I loved. I'd watched too many superhero movies growing up, I realized now. I had unrealistic expectations. It was like reading a romance novel… true love was never like it was in books. It was animated and glossed, sugar coated as if it were a treat on a desert table. It was never what you expected. It was sad, but unfortunately, it was true.

The flames formed an egg around me, cocooning me in its deathly embrace. I could smell my hair burning, feel the heat on my scalp. It wasn't painful—these flames were hot, yes, but they didn't hurt me. Perhaps my magic was good for something... perhaps it made me immune to the burning. Hopefully, I would be dead by the time it burned through the magic layer over my skin. Perhaps the heat resistance would wear away when the layer melted off me. I pinched my eyes closed, hoping, praying for my death to be swift.

At least if I died like this, there was no way that I could hurt anyone with my magic. At least I was the only casualty. No forest fires or spontaneous combustion—mine would be the only life lost. Would it really have been a loss? I tried to think, to hold on to the people who wanted me around. My friends, the headmistress... Where was my family? I didn't have one. Perhaps they knew what I was going to become.

I screamed when the flames ate me whole, the remnants of a ballet skirt dancing at the edges of my vision. The ballerina teased me even in my final seconds.

***

My clothes clung to my body when I woke up and sweat drenched my sheet. I ran to my bathroom, desperate for water. Cool, refreshing water to put out the fire. Water to put *me* out. I nearly stumbled over a step, heaving and clawing at my throat. Was this what a panic attack felt like? Like your insides were trying to escape your body, break free of their fleshy prison? I wanted to cry, but no tears came. Did the heat dry them out? Did they get sick of me and refuse to listen, just like the flames did?

I opened the cold water in the shower, stepping under it without shedding my clothes. My stomach turned and twisted, and a burning sensation rose in my throat. It felt as if a volcano had erupted in my chest, pushing the molten rock up, up, up until it eventually reached my mouth. The vile taste was no better than the sensation of dying in my dreams. I opened my mouth, letting the water of the shower fill it up before I swallowed heavily. I could feel the cold water soothing my throat as it made its way down into my stomach.

On the outside, I barely felt the water; it seemed to evaporate before it even hit my body. Just like Mr. Henry's waves, just like the day I got close to the burnout. Nothing could pierce the heat; nothing could put out the fire.

My tears burned like acid, but I didn't care. The nightmare, that cruel, cruel nightmare had my nerves in shambles. I was afraid of my magic, I knew that. It could sense my fear and now it teased me, bullied me, determined to make my life a living hell. It sure felt like I was in hell… The flames were hotter than normal ones, bigger, brighter. It was exactly what I imagined hell's flames to be.

Finally, the water broke through, sizzling on my skin. It took a few minutes for me to fully cool down, and the cold water was refreshing, like stumbling upon an oasis after wandering the desert for days. I opened my mouth again to take another mouthful of water. It tasted sweeter than it had a moment before, and I kept on gulping it down like it was a drug and I was an addict. I drank until my stomach ached and cried out for me to stop. Only then did I turn off the water and get out the shower. Only then was I satisfied and drenched enough to keep the fire away for a little while.

Only then did I feel safe enough to leave the security the water gave me, and head back into my room.

I didn't bother changing before I went back to bed. At least being soaked meant that it would be harder to ignite. There was a clear outline on my bed where my body had been—a perfect, black burn. At least I hadn't burned through to the mattress.

Not bothering with changing the sheets, I got back into bed, shivering. Good, I wanted to be cold. I wanted to freeze. I looked at the ceiling above my head, at the stars I had painted on it when I was a child. They had glowed in the dark, once upon a time, but the glow had long since expired. They were only white stars on a black ceiling, now. I'd been sleeping on this same single bed since I was a child. In fact, the entire room was the same. I wasn't one for decorating. It was plain, generic, like something a video game auto-generated for an NPC.

I didn't sleep again that night; instead, I lay in bed, staring at the ceiling and wondering how in the seven hells I was going to control this damned magic.

CHAPTER 5:

Past

I knocked on the large oak door in front of me. It was an ornate door, with a golden knob and hinges to match. Intricate designs were carved into the wood, designs similar to those on the rest of the doors in the southern "class" side of the academy. The doors on this side gave the person outside a glimpse of what they could expect to find behind the door.

The headmistress's door had a large carved elk, with smaller animals at both sides. Some were gazelles and some were birds. Those represented the teachers. Before them was a crowd of rabbits, otters, squirrels, and anteaters. Those were the students. The elk stood above them all, bigger and more detailed than the rest. This was the headmistress, beautiful and ethereal. It was an accurate representation of the real headmistress. The doors were the only remnants of the old building, and looked out of place in the modern hall. I tried to imagine the doors in the building's original state, tried to imagine the hallways as they were supposed to be—like the ones in the west wing, stone and marble with ornate windows. Yes, that suited the doors much better.

"Come in," a feminine voice called, and I stepped inside.

The headmistress' office was as ornate as the door, with large oak furniture and golden finishes. Books lined every single wall, and on the desk sat a slim, blonde woman. She didn't look a day over 40, even though she'd been around before any of the teachers. Some teachers even told the students that the headmistress was at her post when they had attended the academy, as well.

She was an ancient beauty, but her face didn't give any inclination of her actual age or wisdom. But her eyes, her chocolate eyes held a wealth of stories. It was easy to miss her ancient status, but one look into her eyes told you enough. They shone like stars at midnight, telling tales and sharing wisdom. Her eyes were the only things that told a person of her age and it was unsettling. It didn't match her pixie-like face, with her sharp chin and small nose. It didn't match her long curly hair that shifted from gold to platinum, depending on the light. It didn't match her slim figure and the heels she favored — higher than I could ever sport.

"You look like you've seen better days," she said, her face softening.

I sighed, taking a seat in the large, uncomfortable chair in front of her desk. She always knew when something was bothering me. Not the usual, teenage drama, no. She could tell when there was something deeper, something in my soul making me unhappy. That was why she sent for me before school. She wanted to talk, but I wasn't sure how I felt about talking. Not after last night. Not after the dream that consumed me. The images of flames, of teasing skirts, had wormed themselves into my mind ever since. I couldn't think of anything else. I couldn't even eat my breakfast without my mouth tasting like ash after every bite I took. The toast was in the trash now, along with Wendy's uneaten cereal.

"I can tell that you don't want to talk," she continued, then came to sit on the chair next to mine. She turned to face me, her legs stretched out in front of her. Those legs took up most of her body, and if she were cast in some big, Hollywood movie, she would have portrayed the fashion model.

"How can you tell these things?" I asked, annoyed that she knew so much.

She chuckled. The sound was sweet, like a birdsong. "I raised you, Cornelia. I know every hint, every twitch, every facial expression. Now, tell me, what's got that pretty face of yours in a scowl?"

I instinctively slackened my face, not having realized that I was scowling until she'd pointed it out. It was an annoying habit of mine. Wendy always said I had a resting bitch face. I didn't tell her that she had one, too.

"Do you think my parents had the same magic as me?" The question was out of my mouth before I could stop myself, before I could think further. This was her one rule, the one thing she told me not to ask about: my parents. She said that she didn't know anything and it broke her heart every time she had to tell me. This time, the question didn't seem to upset her, though. Instead, she smiled softly.

The headmistress tilted her head to the side, considering the question. "It's impossible for me to say. I found you in the remains of a burned-down building, and you were only seven at the time." I knew this story inside-out, but I let her go on regardless. It was the story she hated to tell, but once she started, there was no stopping her.

"It's possible that a family member started the fire, yes. But there were no other remains in the building. It was completely empty, save for you," she explained. "You kept mumbling something about losing your mom and sister, but you said nothing else. Nothing to give any indication of where they might have been or who they were. I tried to track down any possible family, but there was no one to be found. I sensed that you had a great power within you that you wouldn't have gotten until you reached the age of nine. I sensed your flames lingering below the surface, waiting for the day they could be free. I knew that I had to help you control them — or, at least, teach you about magic. If you ended up in the system, who knew how wild your magic could have become? So, I adopted you."

Yes, she adopted me. She raised me at the academy, her study becoming my little room as she filled my childhood with knowledge that was far too complicated for my young brain to comprehend. She was too intelligent, too all-knowing for it to ever have crossed her mind that the information she was sharing made no sense to a child. I didn't have the heart to tell her that as a kid, and so I'd worked extra hard to learn it all. And I didn't have the heart to tell her that now, either.

There was nothing she could tell me of this story that I didn't already know. I didn't know why she felt the need to tell it to me yet again, not after I'd asked her a simple question.

"You aren't answering my question," I pointed out, an eyebrow raised.

She sighed. "No, I suppose I am not. The thing is, Cornelia, I cannot tell you where you come from or what gave you the power that you have. Fire magic, it is so incredibly rare. In most cases, it's not hereditary—it's not something that gets passed down. When I was a child, my mother used to tell me that the elemental magics were gifts from the gods. She said that each god came down to Earth to give a selected few a droplet of their own powers, the powers that kept the world alive. The sun goddess herself gave the power of flames, but she grew tired of the human race misusing her magic so much that she stopped giving her gift as often. Now, there is only one, maybe two every 100 years."

"Fiona and me," I mumbled, and she nodded.

"Fiona's magic was too much for her to handle."

"My magic is too much for me to handle," I said, suddenly finding the hem of my skirt incredibly interesting. I examined it closely, avoiding eye contact.

"Oh, honey," she cooed, her small hand on my back. "You are so much stronger than you give yourself credit for. You can control the flames; you can control your magic. You possess a power that even I don't fully understand. You just have to stop being afraid of it and get to know it."

"Mr. Henry said a similar thing." I shrugged. "I don't know what that's supposed to mean."

"Ah, yes. I hear that you have finally accepted his offer to help you." I opened my mouth to ask her how she knew, but she cut me off before I could say a single word. "I know everything, Lia; I have known of your visits to the forest for months. Who do you think sent Mr. Henry to keep an eye on you in the first place?"

"You knew and you didn't stop me?"

"I knew that you needed a place to practice, and it couldn't be in the academy. I let you go out there but I always kept an eye out for danger. Flames are so easy to lose control of, as you already know."

I sighed, defeated by the fact that I wasn't nearly as sneaky as I would have liked to believe I was. "So, what now?"

The headmistress frowned at me. "I am not going to punish you, if that's what you're asking. You're going to practice with Mr. Henry, and sometimes I might join in to help you. I couldn't before, because you didn't want help. But now that you're open to the idea, now that you realize how dangerous your magic can become, now I can help you."

"You should have forced me into practicing with you," I told her.

The headmistress laughed. "I cannot force you to do anything you don't want to, Cornelia. Especially not where your magic is concerned. Magic can feel the unhappiness of its caster. And that's when it gets dangerous. It's trying to protect the witch or warlock and grows out of control to get rid of anything that might be causing the discontent. With normal students, the magic is easy to suppress. It's easy to block or snuff it out before it gets dangerous. Your magic, though... It will go to extreme lengths to protect you and itself."

"Protect me? I feel like it's trying to consume me, instead."

"Perhaps that's because you are causing your own unhappiness." The headmistress got to her feet, straightened her pencil skirt, and held her hand out to me. I took it and stood. "You are trying to suppress your magic, and that is why it is retaliating. It's going against you because it sees you as the enemy. You do everything in your power to get rid of it, to hide it away and ignore it, when actually, it should be a part of you. You have split yourself from the magic, and now your magic is confused. It knows it has to protect itself but without you being one with it, it is attacking you instead."

Was what she said true? Of course, it was true, she was all-knowing. She knew magic better than magic knew itself. She wasn't the head sorcerer of her generation for nothing. What she said was true, but I had no idea how to fix it. How could I become one with the very thing that was trying to consume me? How was I supposed to become the flame? It terrified me, and I had no idea where to even begin.

"How do I do this?" I asked.

The headmistress smiled. "You need to get to know your magic first."

CHAPTER 6:

MEAN GIRLS

The cauldron in the middle of the classroom boiled and bubbles escaped, flying out and popping overhead. It was a sweet scent—not the scent that came with magic, but one that came with a certain potion that helped clear the mind. There was an overwhelming fragrance of hibiscus and lavender, and it made the back of my throat burn. There was an abnormal amount of honey in the cauldron, too, which made for a very interesting aroma. It wasn't unpleasant, but it certainly wasn't something I wanted to get used to.

Mrs. Finnick, the potions professor, was a frail old woman with glasses as thick as her thumbs. No one liked her very much, and she had the tendency to ask questions in tests about things that didn't even exist. She often said that modern-day witches didn't deserve to be called witches and did everything in her power to prove her point. She never succeeded.

Her mouse-brown hair was pulled into a tight bun and her crooked fingers pointed toward a kid at the back of the group of students who circled around the cauldron. "You, in the back," she croaked, her voice high-pitched. "You must know these potions back to front. Otherwise you wouldn't be standing there, chatting the entire time. Mind telling me what the secret ingredient is?"

Even though the kid hadn't actually spoken during her lecture, he didn't give up the opportunity to backtalk. It was how this class usually went. Mrs. Finnick called someone out for something they didn't do and the kid lost his patience with her, typically buying him detention.

"If I knew the secret ingredient, it wouldn't be a secret ingredient, now would it, Mrs. Finnick?" he retorted.

The professor's eye twitched and for a moment I was certain she was going to grow talons and rip the kid's throat out. "You think that you are very clever, don't you, Mr. Harris? You think that this is all a joke?"

"This class is a joke," he said, crossing his arms. "It's not as if you actually teach us anything. Nothing we know about potions was taught by you; it was read in the tomes in the library."

He was telling the truth. We hadn't really learned anything in this class. There was an entire potion section in the library that most of us had nearly memorized, just so we could pass the nearly impossible tests that Mrs. Finnick gave us. If we flunked potions, we had to spend another term in her class, and no one wanted that.

I'd spoken to the headmistress about Mrs. Finnick, but she didn't want to hear it. She'd said that this miserable old broad was the best potions master in the country. That didn't help much, if she didn't want to teach any of us. I'd said as much to the headmistress as well, but she had dismissed it right away. No one wanted to hear how awful this woman was, and it was infuriating.

"You've just bought yourself a week's worth of detention, Mr. Harris. Does anyone else feel like joining him?"

The class was silent. Detention meant extra time with her, being lectured and scolded to her heart's content. No one wanted that, but she seemed to enjoy it so much that she was determined to get at least two students in detention per week, no matter how innocent they might have been in the situation.

I bit the insides of my cheeks, forcing myself not to say anything. The fire in my belly burned but I forced it to stay right there. It wasn't going to come out in a room full of students. That would have been catastrophic. Wendy elbowed me in the ribs, letting me know that she was thinking that same thing as I was.

She had been there, the day of my burnout. She had been there the day I'd nearly set the entire forest on fire. She knew that this unfairness, this cruelty was something that triggered me. Like everyone else, I despised mean people, but I supposed it was different for all of us. Margot, the tramp across from me in the circle, seemed very satisfied with herself. She enjoyed seeing others suffer. She winked at me, and Wendy flipped her the bird. Some people enjoyed mean people, as long as the mean people weren't mean to them. I, on the other hand, knew what it felt like to be on the receiving end of a bully's wrath. I knew the anxiety; I knew the humiliation. And I couldn't bear seeing anyone else in that situation.

"That's what I thought," she said, smiling as if she was actually proud of her childish behavior. I could never understand that; people who became teachers who didn't actually enjoy teaching.

They went out of their way to make the students' lives miserable, and for what? We already hated school. No sane-minded person would actually enjoy school more than having free time, so why did they have to make it extra horrible? Why did they feel the need to terrorize kids that were a third of their ages? Perhaps they felt small, lonely, and powerless. Perhaps picking on people who couldn't defend themselves gave them a thrill. It was cowardly and weak.

I couldn't wait for graduation to come, so I could finally talk back to Mrs. Finnick without feeling her wrath for a week afterwards. There were a lot of things I wanted to tell a lot of teachers, tell a lot of students, but now was not the time. I had to hold my head down, to keep as much peace as possible. There were too many people who hated me, too many things that could go wrong. Too much fire in my belly that could hurt too many people. Too many things for too little satisfaction.

The rest of the class went by at a snail's pace, as it usually did, and when the bell rang for lunch, the students couldn't get out fast enough. It was only outside of the classroom that I was grabbed and pushed against a wall, two icy blue eyes glaring into mine. I found myself vaguely aware of my imperfect eye color. It wasn't like Margot's, perfect and uniform. No, my eyes were nothing like that. It was as if whoever made me couldn't decide on which color would be best, so they'd added all of them instead of one.

"I bet you like Mrs. Finnick picking on everyone," she hissed, her face too close to mine. I could smell her chewing gum. "Do you find it satisfying to see her torment everyone else?

You know, just because you hate your life doesn't mean you have to stand by to see someone else make us hate ours. If I were you, I'd go to the headmistress and rat on that bitch."

Margot had her forearm pressed to my throat, threatening to steal my air. I didn't fight her. What was the use? Everyone would just hate me more if I hurt their precious Margot. She was untouchable.

"I find it funny that you think I have any power to get Mrs. Finnick reported." I wasn't panicking. I knew how this went already. Margot was very uncreative with her bullying methods. It was always the same… the same insults, the same rumors. The feeling in my gut was not fear or panic, it was resentment. I hated Margot, and I wanted to burn her arm until it blistered. But I didn't, because I knew that once I did fight back, everyone would be talking about it. I didn't want to be the subject of any more rumors.

Margot's thin lips spread into a cruel smile, her pearly whites on display. "Everyone goes on and on about how powerful you are, but I don't see that power. I've never seen that power. I think it's just a lie that you made up to seem special. But guess what, loser, you're not. And—"

"Get your hands off her, Margot," Damien's voice boomed from the crowd, and the next thing I knew, his head was visible next to hers as he whispered in her ear. "The only loser here is you. Don't you understand that Lia can turn you to ash with the snap of her fingers? I've been told that it's not a very pleasant death."

Margot's nostrils flared as she let go of me and turned to Damien. He didn't back off, didn't so much as blink when sparks circled her hands. "Are you sure you want to talk to me like that, Jensen?"

Damien grinned, making an expression that I have never seen on his face before. It was on the brink of madness. He grabbed her hand, and as soon as he did, the sparks disappeared and she yelped. Didn't she know about his magic? Of course, she did, but she didn't think it could actually affect her. She was the most powerful sorceress in the school—according to her followers, no one could stop her. No one but Damien.

"Get the hell out of here, Margot," he spat. "And leave Lia alone. She didn't do anything to you, and it's time you leave her the hell alone before I do something to you, instead."

"Is that a threat?" There was a crowd now. I shifted uncomfortably. I didn't fight back for this reason. I wasn't afraid of Margot; I wasn't afraid of anything except myself. I wasn't afraid of anything any of them could do. It was what I could do that was the real problem.

"Damien," I started, but then there was a hand on my arm, pulling me to the side. It took me a moment to realize that it was Wendy, her scowl looking like something that nightmares were made of.

"Let him do this," she suggested. No one seemed to notice us disappearing into the crowd—every eye was on Damien and Margot.

"He shouldn't be fighting my battles," I protested as she led me out of the front doors of the school. She didn't seem to notice the drizzling of rain.

"Exactly." Wendy turned on me, poking me in the shoulder

with her index finger. "*You* should be fighting your battles. It's not our job to get you out of it."

"I never ask you to—"

"Lia, you're our friend and we love you. You think we'll just stand by and let that witch torture you? Never in a million years will we let that happen. Frankly, I find it insulting that you think we won't jump in. And it's fine, it is. But it would be nice if you fought with us. It's your war, your battle, your enemies. We will stand with you, but you have to start standing up for yourself. You're the most powerful witch in this damned place. Are you just going to allow Margot to push you around like this?"

I glared at Wendy. "I know that I can take her all by myself, Wendy, but you might want to think about the reasons I don't do it instead of the reasons I should. My magic is out of control, and if our fight has to turn into a duel, I will kill her—and probably most of our audience. I am not getting my magic stripped because I was an idiot. I am not getting it stripped without me at least trying to keep it under control."

"Maybe your magic is out of control because you don't protect yourself." She shrugged.

"What?"

"Your magic has to protect you because you don't," she explained.

"You sound like the headmistress," I huffed.

"Then maybe I'm right." Wendy looked over my shoulder to the entrance of the academy, then back at me. "Damien isn't going to be around forever to protect you, and if he doesn't, your magic will. You have to stand up for yourself, Lia. Margot gets away with that stuff because she knows you won't fight back. She knows that you won't hurt her and maybe, just maybe, you should. Give her a blister or two—hell, burn her bottle-blonde hair off. And if you don't want to use your magic, use the fire in your belly, instead. Tell her what you want to tell her and make her back the hell off."

"It's not that easy," I insisted.

"It really is."

CHAPTER 7:

LIBRARY

The library was a quiet place.

Not because of the constant shushing of the librarians, like we were used to in movies, but because there weren't many students who ever bothered hanging around. If it wasn't for research on Mrs. Finnick's class, the library was mostly barren.

But I spent a lot of time in the library. Not only did it have every book my heart could desire, but it also had peace and quiet—something not even my tower had when Fiona was around. Fiona avoided public places as much as possible and until she found out that the library wasn't as crowded as I always claimed it was, she'd leave me alone whenever I was there.

I greeted the librarian behind the front desk with a smile and a quick nod. Her spectacles were impossibly small and sat low on her nose. I doubted that she could actually see through them. She smiled back at me. I was probably the only student who got that reaction from her. Ms. Howard was known for being a broody and generally annoyed character. No one really liked her, but I always thought she was just a little misunderstood. I could relate to her.

Listening to the squeaking of my shoes on the hardwood floor, I found my usual reading nook in the back of the library. It was dark, with only a single reading light to illuminate the whole corner. I tossed my backpack on the unoccupied chair and deflated on the other. This was my thinking corner. Damien called it my "brooding corner," and he wasn't wrong. Many people took showers to brood, but I could never waste that much water. No, I did my best brooding in the library, surrounded by books containing stories far more interesting than my own.

I replayed the events that occurred over the past couple of hours. I had nearly burned the forest down and needed a teacher to help me out of it. I realized that I needed help, then. For years, I've tried to manage on my own, but it was clear that I couldn't. I needed help, and Mr. Henry was as capable as any to do just that. In fact, he was more capable than most. His water magic was one of the only things that could put out my flames—his water and the headmistress' manipulation of air.

But would it be enough? What did he know about my magic, anyway? It was the complete opposite of his. I supposed it was better than not having any help at all. God knew I needed all the help that I could get. I was afraid—afraid of my own magic, and that was no way to live. I refused to be controlled by my own magic. That was not an option. It was either that or be stripped of my magic entirely, and if I had to choose, I'd choose not having my magic at all. Even though I knew the tales of horror that came with that decision.

Our magic was connected to our souls, our very being. It was a part of us, like our own thoughts. I've never seen a sorcerer stripped of magic before, but I've heard it was the most heartbreaking thing to see. I tried not to think about it too much. If I didn't get control of my magic, was I going to be a shell? Was there going to be nothing left inside of me? If it was for the good of the people around me, for the innocent that might feel the extent of my flames one day, would it be worth it? One person doomed to a lifetime of hollowness was a small price to pay for the safety of everyone around me.

At least, that was what I told myself when my mind did wander that far off. It was for the greater good. Why else would the council do such things? They took the most dangerous sorcerers and sorceresses and stripped them of their magic. I doubted they were doing it just for the hell of it. They knew how special magic was to the caster. They knew… I knew… The thought of having my magic stripped, despite how much I despised it, was horrifying. I gulped. No, better things; other things. I had to think of anything else.

Damien, yes… I let my mind wander. It was a maze in my head. It felt as if New York City had taken up residence in my head and built mazes for me to navigate through. It was loud and busy. It was overwhelming.

I found Damien in the maze, grinning at me with that stupid smile of his.

Damien wasn't necessarily handsome, but he had a pretty face. Yes, pretty was a good way to describe it. He had boyish good looks and neatly cut hair styled to perfection. He was the sort of guy you'd see on a football team, had the academy allowed sports—but it was too easy to cheat when there was magic involved.

And he'd stood up for me against Margot. I replayed the scenario in my head. He had taken the heat for me. He'd turned the attention away from me so I could get away. He didn't care who saw him and what they said to him. No, he was just happy to help me out of an uncomfortable situation.

Was Wendy right? Was Damien going to leave one day? Was I going to end up having to fend for myself? The thought made my stomach turn. I couldn't imagine that. Damien was my best friend. Though, best friend was a term used loosely. We were all friends because we couldn't get other friends, and although it was nice having people around who could relate to your problems, these people weren't my friends by choice. At least, they weren't at first. We were forced together, and we'd learned how to tolerate each other.

Damien and Nina were the only ones I felt actually chosen to be my friends. Nina because she was Nina, and that said enough in itself. She was just a general sweetheart. And Damien… Damien felt like my only *real* friend. Fiona was a ghost, and she avoided people as much as possible. I could understand her isolation; I felt like that every day of my life. But it was nice to have a friend that stuck by you, who defended you.

Damien was that friend to me.

I remembered having a crush on him as a child. He was the biggest kid in school, and I knew that he could beat up anyone who tried to pick on me. And he was nice and let me borrow his crayons. As we grew older, I didn't know what had become of that crush. Perhaps there was no such thing as a crush. Perhaps it was all just one giant myth. Maybe I just didn't know what it was.

Many things had faded over the years. Damien was no longer the biggest kid in class and I… I lost control of my magic. Things didn't seem right anymore, and my feelings had changed. Or perhaps they didn't change, perhaps I changed. Perhaps I had grown up and found a whole new meaning in the word "crush." The point was that it was no longer the same. Sure, we flirted from time to time, but that was it. There was nothing more.

Did I want more? Did he want more? Would it have been so wrong to want more? No, it wouldn't have. We were both 18, old enough to think clearly. And I did have feelings for him, I knew. It was just a matter of which feelings those were.

"Lia." His voice rang through my thoughts and I was pulled back to the present.

I felt lightheaded, as if an airplane had landed too fast and my body couldn't process the air pressure just yet. My ears rang and it took me a moment to realize where I was and, in some ways, *who* I was. A wave of reality washed over me, and it was a strange feeling. All I wanted was to get back into that headspace and forget about the reality. Daydreaming about the issues in my life were much easier than actually facing them for real.

When I had full control over my head again, I found Damien lounging on the chair where my backpack was. It was now discarded on the floor.

"That seat was taken," I teased, nodding toward the backpack. The bag was old and had a few tears too many. It didn't feel right asking the headmistress for a new one, so I made do, fixing it with needle and thread whenever a new tear arose. The fact that my sewing skills were worse than my magic skills didn't help the overall look of the backpack, though.

It was pretty much the patchwork of Victor Frankenstein. Sometimes, the threads didn't even match the color of the backpack. Still, nothing fell out of it, and I was able to carry as much stuff around as I wanted. It was a comfortable thing, that backpack of mine. It had memories, it had character. It was special to me. I didn't appreciate the fact that he just tossed it on the floor, but I didn't say anything about it. I knew I was silly to be sentimental about a backpack.

"Is that any way to talk to your knight in shining armor?" Damien raised an eyebrow, his lips twisted into a smirk. Ah yes, he just loved to refer to himself as a knight whenever he managed to get me out of an awkward situation—which happened more frequently than I cared to admit. For a week afterwards, he insisted on being called Sir Damien, rescuer of damsels and dropper of pants, or something equally as stupid.

I gave him a once over, lifting an eyebrow at his blue uniform. It was neatly pressed, but I would hardly refer to it as armor. "You call that an armor, sir knight?"

"You don't know what's beneath this blazer," he defended, and I took my chance, giving him the most seductive smile I could conjure. Damien wasn't overly built, but I had seen him shirtless on many occasions. He wasn't bad to look at, not at all.

"Maybe you should show me sometime," I suggested, feigning ignorance. So, what if I wanted something more than flirting? So, what if this led to something more? Didn't I deserve that? Didn't I deserve that much?

Damien's face flushed and it took me a whole second to burst out laughing. I got a glare from the librarian and I quickly shut my mouth. Damien looked ready to retort, but I interrupted him.

"Relax, Dame," I winked, throwing my legs over the armrest of the chair I was sitting in. "You don't have to show me right now. We wouldn't want the librarian gawking and mis-stamping her books, now do we?"

"You think you could handle what's underneath?" Damien recovered. I chuckled. I enjoyed this. The playful flirting, the jokes between us and us alone. This was nice. This was exactly what I needed after a long day.

"Have you seen my magic?" I pressed, grinning. "I can handle anything."

"You're not very good at handling your magic, though." The blow hit hard, and I tried to take it in the lightheartedness as it was given. Still, it was a little too sensitive, too raw, too real. I immediately lost interest in the flirting. It wasn't his fault; it was mine. I was being overly sensitive.

I tossed a small cushion his way and now it was his turn to laugh. He caught the cushion midair and tossed it back at me. "Am I wrong?" he asked, grinning.

He didn't notice my face fall as replied, studying the tassels on the cushion. "Not exactly, no."

CHAPTER 8:

FAMILIAR

"Close your eyes and find the fire inside," Mr. Henry said, lounging underneath a tree while. He watched me with one eye closed, his hands behind his head.

We were in the clearing where he'd found me the day before. The circle of black grass was still visible where I burned it, and I made a conscious effort to stay away from the area.

"What?" I crossed my arms, my face contorted in confusion. I had switched my uniform out with a pair of jeans and a T-shirt that was a few sizes too big. My feet were bare. That was Mr. Henry's idea. Something about feeling the Earth's power beneath me. I didn't pay much attention to what the reason was; all I could think about was how cold my feet were.

He sighed, throwing his head back to examine the clouds above. It was a drearier day than the day before. "We all have our powers inside of us. It has a home, a place where we can go to find it. Mine, for example, is in the very back of my head. The waves are crashing on a beach, larger and wilder than anything you've ever seen. It's not some tropical getaway, it's a storm—the sort of storm that causes shipwrecks. It's not as calm as the waves I control. It's the raw power, the raw magic that flows through our veins. Once you know where to locate it and what form it's in, it will be easier to control."

"And how exactly is knowing all this going to make it easier?"

"Think of it like the problem child in the family. Controlling the kid is out of the question, because no matter what you do, he or she will go out of their way to disobey. But if you can find the root of the problem, the thing that is making the child act out, it's easier to figure out how to fix it and make things easier for the kid.

"Your fire is the problem child. It's the kid that sneaks out in the middle of the night to go to parties, the child that refuses to do chores or demands an allowance without earning it. This child backtalks and curses like a sailor, doing everything in its power to sabotage the people's lives around him." Mr. Henry closed his other eye, making himself comfortable under the tree. "Now, find the root of your problem and then we can take it further. Sit down, close your eyes and go searching for that fire."

"Why don't they teach us this in class?"

"Because elemental magic is different. It's a physical thing. It's something you can see, smell, and touch. Something like telekinesis or charm doesn't have a physical form. It's easier to control. Even the other elements like earth and air are easier to control than water and fire. Our magic is chaotic and wild, and it takes extra work to master it. No," he said again, waving at me to continue with my searching. "Get to work."

And so, I sat down and closed my eyes. I couldn't see anything, at first. I was just a weird kid sat in the middle of a field with closed eyes. But I could hear and smell everything around me. The damp air, the chirping birds, the rustle of leaves as wind flew through them. I could sense everything around me, but nothing inside of me. I couldn't find the flame. It was hiding from me, knowing what my intentions were.

I sighed with frustration.

"Start from the top of your head and work your way down. Look behind every corner. It could be anywhere. Follow the smell of your magic, the heat. Once you have the scent, you can track it back to the source," Mr. Henry advised, as if he was reading my mind.

I bit back a reply. Instead, I took his advice. If Wendy was right—which she usually was—I couldn't spend the rest of my life avoiding people like Margot. I had to stand up for myself, and to do that, I had to get some control over my magic. Even the smallest amount of control could go a long way. Especially since I had none to begin with.

Starting at the very top of my head, I worked my way down. I imagined my body as a maze, with the core of my magic hidden in the middle. How I was going to get to it, I didn't know yet, but there had to be a way.

I started walking, taking turns that I thought felt right. Sometimes, I had to backtrack and take another path instead. I had a feeling where to go, and the only thing I could do was follow my gut. I had nothing else to go on, anyway.

As I got lower, to my throat to be exact, I caught a scent of smoke. It was very faint, but it was there, nonetheless. I took a deep breath and followed it, taking a few turns that I didn't even notice before I took it. The smoke grew hotter and thicker until I could hardly breathe. I gasped when I realized where I was.

"You found it," Mr. Henry said, now a lot closer than he was before. He sat next to me. His voice was wraithlike in my head, coming from everywhere and nowhere at the same time.

"Yes," I breathed.

"What is it?" he asked. I could hear the excitement in his voice, the genuine interest. I wished I shared that enthusiasm, but I couldn't bring myself to be excited about anything involving my magic. I couldn't be excited about anything that could take my life at any given moment. It was impossible.

I looked at the black rock around me, then up at the perfect, open circle. I could see the sky above, and I didn't dare look down just yet. "I think I'm in a volcano." That would explain the heat. It would explain the boiling sounds, like a hot tub that was just a little too warm for comfort.

"A volcano?" Mr. Henry asked. "Interesting. Explain it to me."

"There are rocks all around me. I think... I think I am in a cave inside of the volcano. I can see the hole at the top."

"And below?"

I gulped and looked down. It took me a moment to form the words to explain what I saw. I'd never seen anything like it. It was beautiful. It was deadly and hot and beautiful. I could feel my physical body starting to sweat. "It doesn't look like lava."

"I didn't think so."

"It looks like fire, but it also looks like liquid. It's as if lava turned to raw fire and kept a liquid form."

"Can you reach into it?"

"Reach into it?" I panicked. "Why would I want to reach into it?"

Mr. Henry's voice was cool in the hot, suffocating air. "This is your body, your magic, Lia. That fire is as much a part of you as your foot or eyes or ears. It is as much a part of you as any other part of your body. Are you afraid to touch any other part of your body?"

"No," I admitted. What a strange question. My body wasn't boiling, my body wasn't liquid fire that wanted to devour the flesh off my bones. The fire looked hot enough to melt bone, as well. It could probably turn my bones to liquid and add it to the sea of fire.

"Then don't be afraid of touching that part, either. Now, reach down and scoop up as much of that fire as you can carry in your hands."

Tentatively, I reached down into the river of fire. I didn't know what I had expected once my hand was fully submerged, but it wasn't this. It wasn't a comforting warmth that flooded my body. There was no overwhelming heat, no fire that threatened to burst from every pore on my body. No, this was peaceful, this was solace, like a warm meal on a cold, snowy winter's day. I had never felt anything like it.

The liquid fire had the texture of silk. It didn't feel like dripping my hand in water or milk, but in melted caramel, instead. It was thick and smelled just as sweet—the sweet scent of magic.

This far in, this close to the source, the magic smelled like candy and I was ready to devour it. I was ready to eat it all. Was I hungry for the power it gave me? Was I hungry for the control? I didn't know, and I knew better than to find out what would happen if I did indulge. I had to remind myself that my magic was too dangerous. Small steps—I had to take small steps.

I reached down with the other hand, too, cupping them together before lifting my hands from the river of flames. It dripped from my hands, dropping on the floor as if it was water. I was awestruck. I had never seen anything so glorious.

"You remember that ballerina you were playing with yesterday?"

I was vaguely aware of my nodding head. "I want you to create her again, but this time, uses the fire from your core. I want you to use it like clay. Make her a little bigger. Add as much detail as you possibly can. Make her as real as you are."

I didn't think twice about what he told me. I didn't have to wonder how I was going to do it. It came naturally, and my hands moved without my conscious thought. Slowly, the body formed, then the head, then the dress. I added the hair, reaching down to get more of the liquid fire when I ran out. I formed her face and gave her little pointed ears. I imagined what my magic would have looked like if it was a person and created every feature accordingly. Sharp, crisp lines, strong features, a permanent scowl. My magic was tough and powerful, and so the ballerina adopted those characteristics. When I was done with her, her little body continued to take shape. She formed little nails and eyebrows of flame. She grew teeth and ballet shoes. Her dress sparkled as if encrusted with a million little diamonds. She was the physical form of my magic, and it was more breathtaking than the river of fire.

"Open your eyes."

I did and was surprised to find that the sun had already set around us. It was pitch black out, no star or light in sight. No light, except the ball of flame in my lap. I gasped when it stretched out like a cat that had just awoken from a nap. The ballerina extended her arms above her head, pointing her toes and rolling her ankles. Her little mouth opened in a yawn.

She was the size of the tip of my middle finger to my elbow. Her dress was nearly as half as wide as she was tall, and her little eyes took up half of her face. Her hair hung in curls around her head—curls that looked exactly like mine.

"What the hell?"

Mr. Henry chuckled, and I turned to him, the little ballerina illuminating him in the dead of night.

"Lia, meet your familiar."

"Familiar?" I looked at the ballerina, who was curling back into her little ball, clearly not having gotten enough sleep. "I don't understand. Familiars are a myth."

"Or so everyone thought," said Mr. Henry before taking a seat across from me, studying the little ballerina.

"Long ago, before there was even talk of cars or cellphones, witches and warlocks were the most powerful beings that roamed the galaxy. There was nothing that could stop them and, as such, there was nothing they feared. The elementals could create creatures of their elements that fought for them in battles. It was said that they took the raw magic in their very core and sculpted these creatures. When the creatures died, that piece of their magic returned to them and they could create more creatures. These creatures were known as familiars. But this ability to create a magical army was too powerful, and the gods stripped it away, afraid of what would become of the Earth if the elementals were able to create more of them. And so, without the familiars to protect the witches and warlocks, the elementals were killed and, soon enough, went extinct.

"The gods were afraid of the elementals rising to power once more, so they only allowed a few witches and warlocks to wield the magic, just enough to keep the balance on Earth." Mr. Henry didn't take his eyes off the ballerina. "I have studied familiars for years and years. I have never been able to create one of my own but you, Lia, you got it right the very first time. You were able to create a familiar in half the time it took the ancients to do. It is said that it took them an entire day to create one, to form it to perfection. Those familiars didn't have minds of their own, they were blind soldiers. But something tells me that this here familiar has much more personality than the whole school combined. This will allow you to get to know your magic, to understand it. Once you get to know the ballerina, you will get to know your flames."

"How did you know I would be able to do this?" It seemed like a load of mumbo-jumbo to me. Why me? Me, of all people? The person who couldn't light a candle without setting a building on fire. The person who couldn't even stand up for herself. How was I the one who'd been given this ancient magic? There had to be another explanation and if I didn't get it from Mr. Henry, then I would get it somewhere else. My stomach turned and bile rose in my mouth. This was too much for me to process.

"I knew when I saw the ballerina yesterday," he said, grinning as if he had just discovered gold. "No one can do that, Lia. Magic doesn't have shapes; it can't take on forms. It is what it is and sometimes, very skilled witches or warlocks can manipulate it, but not always. Usually, it's just raw magic. We always knew you had magic that was rooted much deeper, much hotter than anything we have ever seen. I figured it was worth taking a shot."

"But..." I tried to think of an explanation, of an excuse, of a reason why this worked and why it was a bad idea. I couldn't come up with a single one.

The ballerina opened one eye and glared at Mr. Henry, who only smiled back at her. She huffed, smoke escaping her mouth. It was only then that I realized that she wasn't hot. No, that wasn't right. She was hot, but she didn't burn anything. Her body was one big flame, but it didn't ignite anything around her. She didn't burn Mr. Henry when he reached out to touch her.

Instead, she giggled when he touched her side, swatting his hand away before floating upward to sit on my shoulder. She stretched again, her eyes darting between Mr. Henry and me.

"Are you two going to gawk at me all night or are we going to get some dinner?"

Mr. Henry and I looked at each other, our eyes wide. I had grown up on stories of familiars. The headmistress told me about them every night before bed. Mr. Henry studied them for years. Not once had we heard of a talking familiar, never mind one with her own mind and personality. Mr. Henry had said he thought she might have one, but it was a different thing to see it with his own eyes.

"You can talk?" he asked, a goofy grin on his face.

"Do you see anyone else around? Of course, I can talk." Her voice was high, like what I would expect a pixie to sound like.

"I've never heard of such a thing," he admitted, his eyes fixed on hers.

The ballerina turned her attention to me and smiled. "We are full of surprises, aren't we?"

"We?" I asked, unable to form any other word.

"We are part of the same body, the same system, if you will. I am you, and you are me. We are one and the same."

"Do you have a name?" Mr. Henry asked.

The ballerina shrugged and looked at me again. "I don't know, do I?"

"Not that I know of," I said, shrugging as well. Her little body moved with the movement of my shoulders.

"May I suggest not naming her just yet? Get to know the magic first. It's not a baby that grows into its name. This is different. Every magic has a name of its own, if legends can be trusted. You might want to delve a little deeper into your magic to uncover the original name before creating a new one."

"Why?" I asked and Mr. Henry got to his feet. I followed suit, the ballerina holding on to my wild hair.

"The magic wants to work with you, not for you. Learning its name instead of giving it one will show it that you accept and respect the magic."

"This sounds very complicated," I huffed, looking at the ballerina from the corner of my eye.

"Creating a familiar is the most complicated thing of all, and you've mastered that already," Mr. Henry chuckled before turning on his heels and walking into the forest. "Come on, then," he called out when he noticed I wasn't with him. "I need some light, and that ballerina could be a useful torch."

She stuck her tongue out at Mr. Henry's back.

This was going to be one hell of a ride.

CHAPTER 9:

MIDNIGHT MEAL

I skipped dinner that evening and, despite my greatest efforts, I was ravenous when the 8th bell rang. I had an assortment of snacks in my room, but it wasn't the same as eating an actual meal—it wasn't a steaming plate of food. My stomach still rumbled when the clock read midnight, and so I made my way down the stairs of my tower as quietly as possible.

It wasn't the first time I'd snuck out of my room for something to eat. It was much easier being alone and far away from the other students. Although, usually, I didn't have a ballerina fireball on my shoulder. The light she emitted was useful; it was so bright it illuminated the hallways better than the sun did during the day. But I was a walking torch now, and if anyone came around a corner, I couldn't hide in the shadows like I usually did. No, I had to be extra careful, now. I couldn't risk missing the softest of footsteps. The caretakers roamed the halls at night to make sure everyone was in bed. They stayed mostly in the main dorm, while I was in the west wing with a few teachers. Still, any one of them could leave their room at any moment for whatever reason, and that would mean I was caught. I was as silent as a wraith; I couldn't make a sound.

The familiar and I hadn't spoken to each other since we'd left the clearing in the forest with Mr. Henry. I supposed she was waiting for me to say something, but I was at a loss for words. I didn't know what to make of the situation. It was as if someone had taken my body against my will and dropped it in another life. This familiar was going to make me stick out like a sore thumb. Most of the kids at school wouldn't even know what she was, but why would I walk around with a flaming ballerina on my shoulder? I'd asked Mr. Henry if I could leave her in my room during the day, but he had shaken his head, saying that I needed to keep the bond as close as possible until it became strong enough. Leaving a familiar to its own devices so soon would cause it to lose control and, ultimately, tear down everything in its path to get to its master.

I wanted to tell him that I didn't want it. I didn't want the familiar, I didn't want the attention that went with it and I sure as hell didn't want the power. I was tired of being "special." It wasn't everything it was made out to be. It definitely wasn't what I wanted in life. Any chance of normality had disappeared out the window when he'd made me summon the familiar.

Still, I'd never really had a chance at a normal life even before the familiar. I was already an outcast, the girl with power much bigger than anything else in the academy. The familiar wasn't going to change that. But I wanted to hate it, to resent it. It was easier than accepting I had no chance before her. I liked to think that being normal was still in the cards for me. And I wanted to blame something. It just so happened that the familiar was there at exactly the right moment.

I ducked into the kitchen. I was thankful for the light of the familiar, even though I refused to admit it. I usually bumped my hip on every counter in the place, but with her glow to light my way, I managed to walk around all of it. The kitchen was nothing special, with generic countertops and large sinks. The fridges, that was where I wanted to be. I knelt by the door to the pantry, fishing two bobby pins from my hair before inserting them into the lock. One would think an academy of sorcerers would have learned that putting spells on doors would be beneficial. I was glad that they hadn't figured it out yet, though. Not having spells to get through made getting into the pantry a lot easier. I twisted the pins and when I felt the lock turn, I grinned like the Cheshire cat. My mouth watered. It was going to be a midnight meal, never mind a midnight snack.

"You know," a smooth voice said from behind me. I got to my feet and turned around, my head a little dizzy, as he continued, "sneaking around is much easier without the blinding light."

I glowered at Damien, hoping and praying that he didn't ask what the blinding light was. I had no such luck.

"What is that thing?" He stepped a little closer, the light accentuating his boyish features. I sighed.

"I—" I paused, scowling at myself. If I wasn't always so damn hungry, I wouldn't be in this mess. I should have just stayed in my room until I figured everything out. "She's my familiar."

"Familiar?" Damien repeated, a look of shock combined with confusion on his face. I sighed again.

"Mr. Henry had this idea that I could do it and what do you know? I could. Now I'm stuck having to figure out how exactly I am going to hide it."

"Hide it?" I couldn't read Damien's face now. It was unsettling. "Why would you hide it? It's amazing! You're the only witch alive that can actually summon familiars. Why don't you want to show that off?"

"Because I am already a bloody freak," I pointed out, turning back to the pantry door. I was already fighting my own battles in my head about this topic. I didn't need to fight with him, too.

"What's wrong with that? Being different isn't a bad thing."

"It is when you are me and there's an entire academy of witches out to get you," I snapped. "You don't know what it's like."

"Lia," he started, and I heard his footsteps get louder as he approached me. I turned to face him and found he was already directly behind me. "I *do* know what it's like. I'm at the loner table for a reason, too, you know. Everyone's afraid of me because with me within touching distance, they're all powerless."

I swallowed. I'd never thought about it like that. In a way, everyone at our table was an outcast. Nina, because of her charming magic. People were afraid of her using her magic on them. They were afraid that if they liked her, it was her magic fooling around with their heads. Wendy was depressed and hated her own body. She could change anything around her, every inanimate object, every person's appearance for a short amount of time, except her own. Her magic was useless on herself. What use was being able to change things if you couldn't change the things about yourself that you hated the most? Kids steered clear of her because they didn't know what she would turn them into. The further away they were, the safer they would be. And Patrick? He had the ability to speed up time for certain things. I was certain he could be powerful enough to use his magic on humans, too, but he preferred plants. There was no other person alive who could grow a plant quite as big and beautiful as Patrick. This didn't make him weird, though. He was just a character. He didn't care what anyone thought, and I supposed that was why he sat with us. He found us interesting, and he didn't care who saw him with us.

"Yes, but—" I started, not quite sure what exactly I wanted to say to him.

"No buts," he interjected, his eyes hovering on the familiar. "I expect to see you with her in class soon. I don't think anyone would want to mess with you if they see her on your shoulder. Margot would shit herself."

I chuckled. "I don't think even a familiar could knock her off her high horse."

"True, but we could do with the extra muscle. If we pushed together, we might just be able to knock her off."

We went silent then. I wasn't sure what to say, and I was sure Damien took that as a win.

We stood like that for a moment, and when I couldn't take the deafening silence anymore, turned to the pantry once again. "Are you going to help me, or are you just going to stand there looking pretty?"

"You think I'm pretty?" I could hear the grin in Damien's voice and I pictured it in my mind's eye without even having to look at him. I rolled my eyes.

"Sometimes," I confessed, opening the door to reveal shelves and shelves of food. The fridges were in the very back. "From certain angles." I looked at him over my shoulder. "It also helps that the lighting is so bad."

"You little—"

"Shh, we need to be quiet. Cook Magda usually gets up around one to get herself some leftovers and a loaf of bread."

"An entire loaf?" Damien's eyes grew wide in horror.

"You're a boy," I said, rolling my eyes again as I made my way through the shelves, grabbing ingredients as I went. "You've probably eaten more in one sitting."

"Cook Magda is the size of an imp. She hardly reaches my shoulder. How does she fit an entire loaf in that small body of hers?"

I shrugged. "How should I know? I just look at chocolate and pick up three pounds."

"I think your body is perfect."

My stomach turned and I looked at him. Was Damien actually flirting with me? This was a game both of us could play. "Good, my booty is big just for your satisfaction."

Then he grinned, and despite everything I believed, everything I knew about relationships and how they ruined friendships, I didn't pull back when Damien kissed me. Instead, I wrapped my arms around his neck and pulled him closer.

Whether it was because of my acceptance, or the secret we now shared about the familiar and my midnight excursions to the kitchen, I didn't know. All I knew was that I enjoyed it. I enjoyed being a normal girl, kissing a normal boy. For those few seconds, we weren't sorcerers; we were humans. His touch deprived me of all flames, and I felt cold and empty. It felt good, mundane.

When he pulled away, he was grinning. "Let's get this snack up to your room," he said, looking over his shoulder, his hand still lingering on my arm. "We couldn't want Cook Magna to find us making out in the pantry, now would we?"

"You call that making out?" I teased, opening the fridge door to examine its contents. "I don't know, Dame, you'll have to practice a little bit."

"I'd be more than happy to practice on you."

CHAPTER 10:

A New Habit

I tried not to make visiting the headmistress a habit. I didn't enjoy the lingering stares of the passing students on their way to class. But this week, it seemed as though I just couldn't stay away. I had to talk to her, I had to get advice from her. There was no one else that I could talk to—no one else I trusted, anyway. The headmistress raised me, after all. She was like a mother to me. *Like* a mother, yes. Because she was not my actual mother. That was a wound that I didn't think I'd ever recover from.

I slipped into her office without knocking, not wanting to stay in the hallway longer than was necessary. Especially not with the ballerina on my shoulder. It was still too early for the other students to be out and about. Usually, I wouldn't have been up at this hour, either, but I hadn't slept a wink the previous night. I'd just stared at the familiar, realization dawning on me. An actual familiar. I stared at her while she slept, certain that if I closed my eyes, she would disappear and I would wake up from a cruel nightmare.

If I could summon a familiar, there was a chance that I could control my magic.

It was exciting, but as dawn crept closer, the excitement turned into terror. Yes, I was terrified—terrified of letting the little ballerina out of my sight. I'd heard the stories about rogue familiars, plundering the surrounding villages and eating the livestock. The ballerina didn't seem like the type of familiar to do such things, but she *was* fire, and there were a lot of flammable things in the academy. I was the only one with fire magic. If she did anything, I would be the only one to blame, and I didn't need that on my plate, as well. I had enough to worry about just trying to control my own dreams; I couldn't worry about the damned familiar, too. We still haven't spoken a word. She seemed perfectly content with that, but it gnawed at me. It felt as though there was something I was supposed to say to her. Surely there was something that was said in these situations.

And then there was Damien, who was the right boy at the wrong time. I liked him, I did, very, very much. But now was not the time to distract myself with cute boys. I had to focus on one problem at a time. I had to control my magic before I could even think about a relationship because if I couldn't, my magic would be stripped, and I'd be a hollow shell. I knew that if I developed feelings for someone or something, that was going to be even harder to go through with. I was certain that I would fight, and it was not a fight that was going to end well. No—it was going to end, very, very badly.

"Slow down, Cornelia," the headmistress said, straightening her skirts as she emerged from the back room. This was not her living quarters… Had she expected me, and come here before I did?

It wouldn't have surprised me. I stopped asking such things a long time ago. She was something that no one could figure out. No one could read her. She did things for reasons known only to her, and it was impossible to understand what those reasons were.

"Your mind is all over the place; it's like there's a swarm of bees in my office." She looked at me, tilted her head to one side as she noticed the familiar, then took a step back. "My, you've made a new friend."

The ballerina got to her feet on my shoulders, bowing low. The headmistress bowed her head, as well.

"We need to talk," I said, pointing to the familiar.

"Why, yes, I believe it is a matter to discuss," she agreed, not taking her eyes off the ballerina. I went to sit on those damned uncomfortable chairs again, but she shooed me toward the large couch by the window. I remembered seeing her on this very couch as a child. She had a perfect view of the sunrise from here, and she loved to watch it. "Not this early in the morning. Those chairs are for after the third cup of tea."

"Not there yet?" I asked, grinning. She was a real teapot. I was surprised that she wasn't holding a cup in her hand that very moment.

She gave me a face that told me not to go there, and I grinned even wider as I took my seat. "No, not quite yet. Now," she said and took a seat next to me, turning to face me. It was a casual thing for her to do and it was odd seeing her like this. She was usually too proper, too ladylike to be this informal. "Tell me about her."

So, I did. I told her everything about my session with Mr. Henry and the volcano of liquid fire. I told her about the way I had molded the ballerina, the tingle I'd felt in my hands as I'd sculpted her face. The headmistress didn't say a word the entire time. She listened intently, her eyes darting from me to the ballerina, who had now made herself comfortable on my lap and gone back to sleep.

"Wait, so she can talk?" she asked, her chin pinched between her thumb and index finger. The sun was beginning to rise now, and it made her blonde hair seem as if it was pure gold. I nodded. "And what did she say?"

"Not much," I admitted, looking down at her. Her weight was already a comforting thing. "We haven't spoken since I parted ways with Mr. Henry. She seems content just staying quiet and I don't know what to say to her, to be honest."

"I can imagine that." She nodded. "This is amazing, Cornelia. It is… it's just—" She paused, contemplating which word was the best to use. I'd never seen her like this. She always knew exactly what to say and when to say it, but I could tell this had caught her off-guard.

"I knew you were powerful, Cornelia, but this is on a completely different level," she finally admitted. "I can sense it now that you're here, your power. I think you unlocked something when you summoned her. There's a well of power inside of you that we haven't even begun to explore yet. Everything we thought we knew about you is just the tip of the iceberg."

"You mean, the power that everyone is so afraid of isn't even the real power?" My heart sank. I couldn't even control the power I thought I had, never mind the power that I didn't know about.

A sense of panic washed over me. I knew it would be hard to get a hang on the power I thought I had, but with Mr. Henry,

I'd honestly thought I had a shot. I'd actually believed that there might have been a chance for me not to end up as a husk. But now, when even the headmistress seemed worried, I didn't know if I even stood a chance anymore. The headmistress had once told me that my magic was enough to set the whole school on fire. But now, if it was much more powerful than she thought, was it enough to set a block of house on fire? Maybe two blocks? Was it enough to set an entire town on fire? This was dangerous, this was bad. This was really, really bad.

The ballerina awoke, sensing my discomfort. She looked at me as if she could tell what was wrong. "You're afraid of me," she said, and the headmistress and I both stared at her. "I've known this since the moment you created me. I can sense it, you know; the fear? It makes me uneasy. It makes the magic stir deep within your belly."

"Extraordinary," the headmistress breathed. All I could do was stare at the ballerina, and nod.

"I'm not the one you should be afraid of. I am a part of you. I will never harm you; it is everyone else you should be afraid of. The ones that will want to take me away from you."

The headmistress nodded. "She has a point. If word gets out that you have a familiar, people will come for you."

"People? What people?" There were people that would look for me? And if they found me, what would they do? Kill me? Strip me of my magic? Somehow, I was almost certain that it was the former.

"People who dabble in forces much darker than you or I can even imagine."

The ballerina floated up to the edge of the couch and perched herself on the highest part. She watched the sun through the window. I could have sworn her flames flickered.

"So, Mr. Henry—" I started, but cut myself off, unsure of how to finish my question.

Has he doomed me? Was his fascination with familiars blinding him to the fact that it would put my life in danger? Or did he simply not care? I was angry at him for unlocking this power. I was the one who had to sit with it now, not him. I was the one who had to control it, who had to live with the guilt if anything ever went wrong. He didn't have this burden on his shoulders. I'd had a burden before the familiar, and now that burden was even greater.

"Did only what he thought was best," the headmistress finished, sighing. I could tell she was as annoyed as I was. "And, in a way, it was. This can either save your life or cost everyone else's—it could go either way. But, rather us know the extent of your magic than none of us knowing and you losing control. I couldn't bear losing another student to the flames."

"Fiona?"

The headmistress nodded.

"What happened to her?" I inquired, knowing what her answer was going to be.

"It is not my story to tell." Well, it was worth a shot.

"So, now what?" I asked, tired of the silence that fell between us.

The headmistress looked at me, and the look in her eyes frightened me more than any dark forces that might come my way. "I don't know, Cornelia. I thought I had everything figured out, but clearly, I do not. I will talk to Mr. Henry and get his opinion on the matter. Until then, I would suggest you keep a low profile. I'll excuse you from classes until I have figured something out."

"What is it that you aren't telling me?"

She averted her eyes. "There's an organization that is using every recourse they have to bring darkness on the world. They haven't yet found the tool to delve even deeper into their plans, but now… now, I think they might come after you. You might be the one thing they need to dominate the world."

"I won't help them," I said, instantly on the offensive. "I'd rather they kill me."

"I'm afraid they won't give you that choice, sweet girl. If they catch you, they will make you do their bidding, whether you want to or not. They have ways, dark and devious ways. This is not a matter of want and don't want." She paused and looked out the window. "We have to be smart about this. We have to stay one step ahead of them. No one knows about the familiar yet, which means that word probably hasn't gotten out yet."

"Actually," I confessed, cringing, "Damien saw her last night. He knows."

"Well then, I suggest finding him as soon as possible and making sure he won't tell anyone."

"What about her?" I asked, pointing at the ballerina.

"I don't need a permanent babysitter," she said, crossing her arms.

"You can leave her with me for now. Find Mr. Jensen and make sure he won't talk. Then, you get her after everyone has gone to bed and you stay in your room until further notice. I'll have someone bring food up to your room and tell them to leave it outside your door. Just pretend to be sick and hide her when you open the door to accept it. Otherwise, that door stays shut."

"What am I supposed to do in the meantime?" I asked, my voice whinier than I intended it to be.

"Hope and pray that no one finds out about you."

CHAPTER 11:

SECRETS

It felt weird not having the familiar close to me. It had only been a few hours that she'd been around me, but already it felt as if there was a part of me that was missing now that I was away from her. There was a sort of emptiness in my stomach. It made me feel sick.

I didn't like this. I didn't like this at all. But I couldn't take her with me when I went searching for Damien. The risk was too big. Second period would end soon, and the hallway would be crowded and tearing at the seams. Too many eyes, too many possibilities, too many questions. No, I had to endure the emptiness until I could get back to her tonight. And then I had to figure out how to wean myself off of her. But how? How would I even do that? Was it even possible? Perhaps it wasn't even worth trying. There were bigger things to worry about and, when I did need to control my magic, having her around would be greatly beneficial. Still, this damned empty feeling… it was going to drive me insane.

I didn't know whether or not I should have been happy that I summoned her or to be afraid of it. I had been afraid of my magic for such a long time that I didn't even know how to be afraid of anything else. As a child, there were no monsters under my bed to haunt me. There were no monsters in my closet, either. No, my fear has always been of the monster inside of me—the one made of flame. It was the monster that no caretaker could get rid of, or convince me that it didn't exist. It was as real as I was.

When I'd told the headmistress about it, crying and running to her, getting into her bed with her so she could comfort me, she'd told me that it was going to be okay. She'd never told me that it wasn't going to hurt me, that it was only in my head. It's always been a shadow that loomed over me, knowing that it was a monster that I could never get away from. It was a monster that would chase me anywhere I went, and it would break down any door I closed to get away from it. It was a serial killer that never gave up, no matter how much I begged it to. But now—now, there was something else. Something that the monster that I was so afraid of couldn't stand a chance against, no matter how much it grew, no matter how big it got inside of me. If the headmistress was correct, which she always was, my magic would not be strong enough to resist their power. I would be a slave to them, a weapon. My monster would not stand a chance against their power.

I buried the thought in the back of my head. Being stripped of my magic was no longer my biggest worry. I had to get the image of thousands burning at my hand out of my head. I had to get rid of it like I'd gotten rid of the husk of myself that I saw whenever I thought about my magic being stripped. Fear got me nowhere. It didn't help any situation. Fear made a person do stupid, irrational things.

I couldn't afford to mess up. There was too much at stake. I couldn't even entertain the idea of being captured and used as a weapon. At least now I had some resemblance of control, but if I was controlled by someone else, I would have nothing at all—and that terrified me. It made me want to curl into a ball and weep. But I couldn't. I had to be strong. I had to banish all of those thoughts from my head. It wasn't helping with the emptiness in my belly and the bile that rose in my throat from the separation. It only added to it, and I knew I was going to be sick if I didn't do something. If I didn't push my fear to the back of my mind and focus on the task at hand.

"Damien," I hissed as he passed the janitor's closet. He stopped for a second and looked behind him. I watched him through the crack of the door, opened just enough to see him when he walked past the closet toward his locker. The hallway was full of kids, but I knew his route, and I knew that he liked to walk close to the wall. I knew he didn't like walking in big crowds. I watched his puzzled expression, and when he saw no one behind him, he turned the other way around.

"In the closet, you nit," I said, fighting a smile.

Realization dawned on his face and, without thinking twice, Damien stepped into the closet. The space was small, way too small for two people, but this was what I had to work with. I couldn't wait any longer to talk to him; I had already spent too much time talking with the headmistress after she'd told me to find him. I had spent too much time separating myself from my familiar already, too. I had to catch him before he let anything slip, and this was my best option.

"Lia," he said, rubbing his head after bumping it on a shelf.

There wasn't much room to avoid it, coming in. I was grateful that I was short enough to have missed it when I'd snuck in here. We stood about two feet apart, a broom jabbing me in the back and a tower of toilet paper rolls threatening to tumble over behind Damien. "Not that I don't love being in a confined space with the prettiest girl in school, but I have to ask: Why am I here?"

I ignored his compliment, even though it made me smile slightly. This was not the time for cuteness. This was not the time to relive the memory of the previous night—the kiss, the flirting, the making out. I still wasn't sure how I felt about it, and now was not the time to figure it out.

"You haven't told anyone about..." I leaned in closer to him, whispering my words, "you know?"

"The kiss?" He raised his eyebrow. "No? I didn't think you'd appreciate me going behind your back and telling the whole world about it while you were missing classes. Actually, where have you been?"

"Not the kiss." I smacked his abdomen with the back of my hand. "The other thing. And I've been laying low. Headmistress' orders."

Realization dawned on his face. "Hell no! That's not my secret to tell. Why? Has something happened?" He looked around the closet, trying to find the flaming ballerina in a little room that could hardly fit the two of us. "Has someone taken her?"

"No, nothing has happened." *Not yet,* I wanted to add, but I held back. "I need you to keep it to yourself, okay? No one can know about her. I mean no one, Dame. Not Patrick, not Nina, and not even Wendy."

I didn't enjoy keeping something so big from my friends, but the more people that knew, the better the chance of someone who shouldn't know anything finding out. I was sure the headmistress had spoken to Mr. Henry by now, as well. This was top secret and on a need-to-know basis. If Damien hadn't found me in the kitchen that night, he wouldn't have had to know about the familiar, either.

"I won't tell a soul, Lia," he said. I could have sworn there was hurt in his voice. "What's going on?"

"I can't tell you," I said. I felt guilty, I did. It was awful having to keep something a secret without knowing why it was kept a secret. But I couldn't tell him. Not yet, anyway. I had to figure things out first. I had to get all the information first. I already asked him to keep one secret. I couldn't expect him to keep another. Not when I didn't even know what to do about us, about the kiss.

I didn't want to guilt him into keeping my secrets, and I didn't want to feel obligated to him. The headmistress hadn't said anything about keeping the people that were after me a secret, but I made it a rule myself. The fewer people who knew about anything going on with me, the better. Even if that meant keeping it away from my best friend.

"All I can tell you is that I'm in trouble, but the headmistress is working on it. I just need to stay hidden for a while," I explained. "Only until I have figured out what to do about it all."

"You're kind of freaking me out, Lia."

"I know, and I'm sorry," I said, then took a deep breath. "I just can't risk involving you in something that I myself don't know anything about."

"You involved me the day we met, seven years ago, Lia." He stepped a little closer to me, but I took a step back, shaking my head. The broom did a number on my rib, but I ignored the pain. "I'm sorry, Damien. I'm just sorry."

And then I did the cowardly thing. I did the one thing I despised seeing women doing in movies—I bolted.

I opened the closet door and ran. I didn't care who saw me. I didn't care who I knocked over on my way. I just needed to get some distance between myself and Damien. If I stayed any longer, he would have asked more questions, and then what was I supposed to tell him? I couldn't just repeat myself, couldn't tell him that I couldn't actually tell him just yet, that I was sorry. That was the one thing that made a person feel even worse than they already felt to begin with.

It was easier to run than to face him. It was easier to bolt than to look him in the eye and tell him that I didn't trust him enough. It wouldn't have been in so many words, but that was how he would have taken it. It was how I would have understood it, if I were in his shoes. The problem wasn't that I didn't trust him. I did trust him, more than anyone. But I had to trust the headmistress more, and her orders were not to give him too much information. She had the power to help me, Damien didn't. And if trouble came to find me, I knew the headmistress could hold her own. I knew that Damien, despite every good trait he had, could not fight anyone in a real battle.

CHAPTER 12:

TALKING WITH FIRE

Hours turned into days, and the days became a week.

I had gotten quite familiar with the wall of my tower. I had counted every crack; I had counted every stone. I had grown increasingly aware how dull my room was. There was nothing interesting to look at, and it was starting to get to me. I needed a plant or something, anything, really. I didn't really care what it was, as long as it brought a little color and life into this brown and grey prison cell. I didn't care as long as there was something to distract me from the deafening silence. From the voices in my head that kept retelling the worst stories possible—the stories of how my life would end, of what would happen if I was found. I wanted something to take away the suspense. I'd always hated surprises, even as a kid—especially when someone told me that there was a surprise in store for me. I'd rather they had just kept it to themselves before the surprise actually found me.

Waiting was the hardest part. There were things for me to do, of course. I had access to the Internet, I had books, I had a phone, but there were only so many things you could do before the suspense devoured you whole and there was nothing left to do but study your surroundings, hoping that you would find something interesting enough to distract you from the real problem at hand.

Fiona came to visit me every so often, marveling at the ballerina that had made herself at home on my pillow. I'd tried to make her a little bed of her own, which she refused to sleep in. She wanted to be in bed with me, on my pillow. I didn't mind it much. She radiated a comforting warmth that lulled me to sleep at night. It was something I had come to love about the little familiar.

The ballerina seemed to enjoy the attention. She loved spending time with me, and she adored the hell out of cuddling and laying on people's laps. Fiona seemed to enjoy giving her attention, as well. I didn't know where the ghost went when she wasn't with me. The headmistress assured me that the secret of the familiar was safe with Fiona, so I didn't worry much about it. Still, I wished she visited me more often. I didn't realize how reliant I was on my friends until I wasn't allowed to see them anymore.

I missed them. I was lonely.

The familiar and I had already established a connection. In a way, I thought about her as a child of sorts, and I was certain she felt the same way about me. There was an unconditional love that came with our companionship, the sort of love a mother has for a child. The ballerina and I have also gotten around to chatting. Never about anything that mattered—instead, we spent most of our time reading or watching a television show, then spending hours discussing it afterwards. It was truly extraordinary how much of her own person she was. Even if I weren't around, she would be able to carry herself in any conversation without so much as a stutter. We avoided heavy topics, though. Well, *I* avoided heavy topics. I couldn't be bothered thinking about those things right now. I would only drive myself mad with fictional situations that may or may never happen. Besides, shit was going to hit the fan anyway — what point was there in discussing it now?

"Can you stop pacing?" the ballerina sighed, rolling her eyes as she watched me, head propped up on her hands as she lay on her stomach with her feet in the air. "You're going to thin out the carpet."

"What is taking her so long?" I asked, biting my thumbnail. It was an awful habit.

"There are a lot of things to figure out." She shrugged. "Besides, your assault on that carpet isn't going to make things go any faster. Relax a bit. You have all the time in the world. Why are you spending it worrying when we could be watching Gossip Girl?"

The ballerina had an unhealthy obsession with television dramas. Especially ones that involved damaged characters.

I glared at her. "I'm afraid," I admitted. "I'm so afraid. All of this came out of nowhere. One day I was still getting bullied in the hall, and the next I found out that there might be an evil organization after me? I don't even think everything has sunken in yet. My emotions feel muffled, as if they are being stifled under a heavy blanket. I can't put my finger on it. I know that I'm not reacting the way that I should be, but I don't know how or why."

"I know, I can feel it," she said, turning on her back. She held one foot in the air, stretching her leg.

I turned to look at her fully. "Just how powerful am I?"

She seemed to think it over for a moment. "You remember that volcano? The one you formed me in?" I nodded. "There are about seven of those inside of you. If you combine those, that is your power. This is assuming some of them aren't deeper than others."

I swore under my breath, pushing a hand through my hair only to get it knotted in the curls. Another string of curses left my mouth as I yanked my hand free. This was yet another thing that annoyed me, that frustrated me and felt out to get me at every turn—this jungle of hair on my head. It hung well past my shoulders. I was considering cutting it, but ginger hair, short and curly? I hated clowns enough to fear becoming one. All I would need was a red nose and shoes that were a few sizes too big for my feet. The image made me shudder.

"If they get some sort of power over me," I started, going back to chewing on my nail, "that power is enough to wipe out entire states."

The ballerina shook her head. "There's no way of using all of it at once. It will burn you out. Your body isn't made to wield all of it simultaneously. That's why the gods gave you this body and not one like mine; immune to the flames. If you used all of your magic at once, it would burn you from the inside out. There would be nothing left of you."

"Oh, God," I breathed. My pacing continued.

"But that's why I am here," she continued, and I stopped in my tracks, looking at her. "I possess half of your magic. Imagine yourself being split in two. That's basically what happened to us."

"I don't feel weaker, though. If anything, I feel stronger." I looked at my hands as if I could see the magic within them. I wondered what they looked like, the tendrils of magic that snaked their way beneath our skin. I wondered if it looked like the actual magic, red and fiery. Or did it resemble unicorn hair? Was it while and sparkly? Did it have an ethereal glow?

"That's because you didn't even know about the first volcano before I came along. That volcano got unlocked once you entered it. There are still two more for you to find."

That meant there was more power for me to unlock. That meant the power I felt now, the power that threatened to take my breath away and knock my feet from under me, was not yet everything I possessed. This crippling magic was still not at its peak. I swallowed.

"I don't understand," I said. "How does you being here benefit me?"

"The purpose of familiars was never for us to serve our masters. The legends are wrong. All of them. Some have half-truths, but none really captured the true purpose. When a sorcerer became too powerful, he had the ability to split his magic in half. The one half would inhabit an entity called a familiar, and the other half stayed with him. This was a way for the sorcerers to keep the magic from consuming them. Half the magic wasn't enough to kill them. The other purpose of splitting it in two was that if one half got out of control, the other half could stop it. That half could very easily absorb the blow of the rogue magic."

"So if I lost control..." I started.

"I would step in and absorb the magic," the ballerina finished my sentence.

"What would happen to you, then?"

"I would die," she said, matter-of-factly. "And I would take my half of our magic with me."

"You would die for my mistakes?"

"Don't think of it like that. I am a part of you." She got up and walked to my pillow, making space for me to lie down. I did, and only then did she continue. I stared at the dull stars on the ceiling.

"Ultimately, I am an extension of you," she went on. "I will not be killed; I will be sacrificed. It's a measure that your own magic has put into place, a way of protecting itself. It's a way of protecting you. It's your magic's job to protect its master, and despite what you might think, you are its master. You are my master."

"What do you know about what I think?" I challenged. I didn't address the fact that she had called me her master. It made me feel like a slaver.

The ballerina smiled. "Oh, Lia. Have you forgotten already that I told you that I am a part of you? I have heard every thought, every doubt. I know every fear and want that is in your heart. I know that you are afraid of the magic inside of you." She tilted her head to the side in quiet contemplation before adding, "Well, less now than in the past. You have a new fear now. But it's not the Dark Brotherhood that you are afraid of, is it? It is what they will make you do to your loved ones that is actually scaring you. You are afraid of your relationship with the boy. You are afraid that it was ruined by the kiss, that he will treat you differently now. You are afraid because you don't know what you feel, and you know enough about feelings to know that it is not a good sign. You do not feel the same way about him as he does about you."

"Okay, that's weird."

"It's true," she said with a shrug. "I am the part of you that knows all of these things. I am the part of you that helps find solutions to your problems. I am your magic. It's my job to protect you, mentally and physically."

"How do you know how he feels about me?"

"Everyone knows—and deep down, you know, too. You just choose to ignore it as much as you possibly can. Think back, Lia. Think about the way he acts around you, the things he does. Do you think it's a coincidence that you end up sitting next to him every time you eat together? Do you think he would defend anyone else in your group like he does with Margot on a weekly basis? He kissed you, not the other way around. He made the first move, which means that he is into you."

"Shit," I breathed. "I don't have the time or energy for this. There are other things on my plate. I can't think about what to do with him right now."

"Thinking about what to do doesn't address the actual problem at hand. It essentially only makes you overthink things. Sometimes, it's better to just let things run its course. Let the situation play out on its own and then just act in the moment. You assess everything—every single situation. You've mapped out every scenario. You, my dear Lia, are a control freak."

"I am not a control freak," I defended, crossing my arms.

The ballerina laughed. "You're frustrated that you can't control your magic, and therefore you have to control everything else in your life."

"Can we talk about something else?"

"Not yet," the ballerina said, then floated toward me until her eyes were the same height as mine. I stared into the void of light. "You need to hear this, first, because you are going to drive us both insane with your constant worrying. You cannot control fate. You cannot control what will happen, what will come, or how it will come. It will come when it is ready, and it will come regardless of whether or not you are. It is your choice how you react to it, but ultimately, it won't make any difference in the outcome because things will end the way they're supposed to end. It's the way fate works, and the way destiny is laid out."

"So, I just sit back and let it happen?"

"That's not what I said. You will fight when the time comes. *If* the time comes. It's impossible to know. You will fight until you win or you lose. But that is something to worry about when you get there. It doesn't help to have planned out your moves, because your moves rely on you knowing the moves of your enemy — and trust me, Lia, you do not comprehend the power of your enemy."

I swallowed. "And how do you know it?"

"I can sense it. I can feel it in the flames that make me. It's the same way I can sense what a creep Damien is. The earth is crying, screaming for help, but nothing is coming to its rescue. The Dark Brotherhood is juicing the earth for every droplet of magic it possesses, and corrupting it. They are turning it into something darker, crueler. It's a fowl type of magic, I can feel it. It's the sort of magic that would make my stomach churn, if I had one. I can't even imagine the stench of it. Thank the gods that magic isn't close enough to smell. Not yet, anyway. I can feel sinister forces at work in the shadows, and I can feel it here, too. It's not as raw and evil as the magic I can sense far away, but it is darker than the rest. I can't put my finger on it, but it is here."

I ignored the jab at Damien. "In the academy?"

She nodded. "I believe that is the reason why the headmistress has told you to keep to yourself. I think she's trying to find the source, but it's impossible. There's a veil over it, dulling the foulness of it. There's a spell on it that averts the eye as soon as it gets too close. The headmistress is trying to determine some way to break through, but she hasn't found it yet. I believe that is the reason why she is taking so long with news. She can't go snooping if there are eyes everywhere."

"This is all a giant shitshow."

The ballerina laughed. "That awful magic probably smells like it, too."

CHAPTER 13:

SILENCE WITH A FRIEND

Sometimes, it felt good to just sit quietly with a friend. It was good to lay on your bed, feet propped up against the wall, staring at the ceiling next to someone you trusted with your life. Sometimes, life became too much—sometimes, it was too much for our minds to handle, and then it was just good to be with someone. Not to talk, not to vent, gossip, or cry. No, you just had to be with someone, sharing stolen ice cream straight out of the tub.

One of the benefits of Fiona being a ghost was that she didn't eat, which meant there was more ice cream for me. Fiona was no help when I pushed the bed against the wall, but she was a little deviant and got me the ice cream from the fridge. I didn't know how she managed to sneak it past Cook Magna.

Fiona once explained to me how her ghostly powers worked. She could manifest just enough power in the world of the living to pick up small items. She could go completely invisible, but whatever item she was holding would not follow her visible body to the limbo world where she resided. She basically had three forms in the land of the living; the invisible form, the visible form, and the form that could touch things.

That was the closest form to her living body she could get. She was still almost completely transparent, but she had a physical weight, a mass.

I looked at my mismatched socks next to her pale feet. She was barefoot. It always struck me as weird that she was basically wearing a ball gown but went barefoot all the time. I didn't ask her why this was. I had a feeling it had to do with her death—the details of which she was not yet ready to share with me. I accepted that, though. She didn't have to tell me anything she didn't want to. She'd promised that she would tell me one day, and that was enough for me. I just hoped that day would come before I met my inevitable end.

Whether it would be by my own fiery hand or the hand of someone who wanted to control my fire, I didn't know. What I did know was that my end would come soon, and I didn't want to die without knowing what happened to Fiona.

"Everyone is wondering where you are," Fiona said as she adjusted herself on the bed. Her head was hanging off the side of the mattress. I was luckily short enough that it was only the tip of my head and my hair that dangled off the edge. "Your friends are feeling left out. Damien is trying to calm the storm, but he can only do so much."

"Isn't the purpose of this exercise to stay completely and utterly silent?" I was annoyed that she'd brought it up. I didn't want to think about anything outside of this room. I especially didn't want to think about anything that involved fire, friends, or an unknown evil.

"Hey, you said *you* weren't going to talk. I didn't make the same promise." She rolled her eyes and flicked my nose. I glared at her.

"Oof, someone has a mean scowl today. Okay, okay," she said, throwing up her hands in defeat. "I'll be quiet."

"Finally," the ballerina said from the head of the bed. The pillow was indented where she lay and she stretched out, getting comfortable again. I wished I could sleep as much as she did.

"That one is basically a cat, isn't she?" Fiona pointed toward the ballerina with a thumb.

I snorted as the ballerina gasped. "I am *not* a cat." Her nap was forgotten now, and she sat up, crossing her arms and glaring at Fiona. She didn't take kindly to being referred to as a pet, it seemed.

"It's not a bad thing," Fiona said, a grin on her face. "Cats are stereotypically a witch's familiar, isn't that right? It would make senses for you to be cat-like. You have the grace, the attitude, the need for attention only when you want it and everyone else be damned."

Fiona wasn't wrong. My familiar was basically a flaming cat in the shape of a ballerina. Some nights, I could even swear I heard her purr as she cuddled into the crook of my neck. She wanted constant attention, but only when she felt like it. You couldn't take it upon yourself to pay attention to her. She demanded attention, received it, and then went back to sleep. That was how she worked.

I had grown quite familiar with her patterns.

The ballerina huffed, laying down again and turning her back to us as we giggled. I could hear mumbling coming from her tiny form, as well. It was hard to tell what she was saying, but her curses were the most colorful thing in the room.

"I'm sorry I haven't been around much," Fiona said after our giggling had died down. "The headmistress has me on spy duty. What's the use of having a ghost in your academy if you can't use her to spy on people, right?"

I sighed. It seemed like the conversation was headed toward the inevitable, anyway, so I asked, "Have you found anything?"

Fiona shook her head. "Nothing we didn't already know about. The Dark Brotherhood is on the rise, and it's not looking pretty. The council has thrown a blind eye their way, and it's meant that the Dark Brotherhood had all the freedom in the world to plot."

"Surely the council will be held accountable," I said. My hands rested on my stomach, and I could feel it turn.

Fiona snorted. "By who? The council's council? No, they had people on the inside, and once you have someone in the council, you're pretty much free to do whatever the hell you want. Including stealing the Earth's resources to build an army of magical soldiers. Even if I can find the rat inside the council, there is nothing we can do. He or she has already brainwashed the rest of them. Even the headmistress can't go up against that. She would be stripped of her role in the magic community for even suggesting that the council was dirty. It wouldn't matter how true it was, the council wouldn't stand for any propaganda that went against them. If the image of the council was hurt, the rest of the magical world would rise against it. Without a council, there will be no laws. The council has been the source of too much suffering in the past. The people wouldn't want a new council. They'd rather eliminate any sign of resistance before it got out there."

"So, where does this leave us?" I asked, dreading her answer. I couldn't imagine having to stay in this room for much longer. I couldn't stand the thought of being useless for however long it took to find something useful. If they haven't found a single piece of evidence, any clues in the week I have been on lockdown, I doubted they were going to find anything of use in the weeks to come. We had to re-strategize. We had to rethink the situation.

I'd missed out on practice with Mr. Henry—practice that I needed to get a hold on my magic. If they got to me, I would be a sitting duck. At least if I had some sort of handle on my magic, I could defend myself. Things had to be reconsidered and hard choices had to be made. I'd have to talk to the headmistress again, so we could reevaluate the situation together.

I would go to her office in the morning. I would list my concerns and maybe, hopefully, we could find some solution that didn't involve me being trapped in the tower like Rapunzel.

"Exactly where we started."

CHAPTER 14:

STRANGER DANGER

The ballerina and I practiced magic in the confines of my tower. We used the bathroom, based on the logic that there were fewer flammable objects in there. Besides, if things got too hot, I could just hop in the shower and cool off.

But I wanted to practice with Mr. Henry. Not that I didn't enjoy practicing and delving deeper into my magic with the ballerina; that wasn't the case at all. I just missed human interaction. I missed the fresh air. And sure, cracking a window was an option, but it wasn't the same. It wasn't the same as feeling the sun or the rain on your skin. It wasn't the same as breathing in the fresh, open air. I also wanted to show Mr. Henry what I had learned. I wanted to tell him about the volcanos and the role of the familiar that everyone had gotten so terribly wrong all these years. I wanted to tell him all of this, but I couldn't.

Because there was still no word from the headmistress, and it was getting to me. I was still planning on seeing her in the morning, but I had hoped, in some small part of my brain, that I would get news before I had to go to her. Some small part of me hoped that all hope wasn't gone. I was an idiot for doing so, though. I was setting myself up for disappointment.

I had taken the ballerina's advice to heart and I tried to focus on other things. I focused on my magic mostly, channeling it and bending it to my will. For the most part, it went well, but in the dead of night when I couldn't sleep and there was nothing to do but think about what the future held, it got to me. It really did. I could see that monster I had created as a child to give a face to my magic when I closed my eyes. I could see that monster attempting to protect me from an assault by a bigger monster with pointier teeth, but ultimately failing. I saw the monster's chest still and the other monster grinned at me, mouthing that I was next. My dreams were haunted by the monsters and I didn't know what to do, other than stay awake as much as I could. It was the best I could do until I spoke to the headmistress.

Still, I couldn't figure out what was taking the headmistress so long. Even after the talk with Fiona, I had been thinking about what could possibly be holding her up. Her, of all people? She was an ancient, a sorceress who had the world's knowledge tucked away in her head. Surely it wasn't too difficult for her. And if it was… where did that leave me? What did that mean for my future? The headmistress had infinite knowledge and contacts; what did that say about the Dark Brotherhood? What did it say if even the headmistress' resources couldn't figure anything out?

"Focus on the candle, Lia," the ballerina instructed, and I glared at her. She didn't seem affected by the look on my face. I suppose she was used to it by now. I was a constant fuse just waiting to be lit. I was starting to get on my own nerves, but I didn't know how to stop it. I didn't know where to begin.

"I am focusing on the candle," I hissed, my eyebrows creasing as I stared at the wick of the candle. It was still snow white; it was still unburned.

The ballerina rolled her flaming eyes, crossing her arms as she pointed toward the wall. "Tell that to the wall behind the candle."

I huffed. She was right. I knew she was right, but that didn't mean I was going to admit as much to her. I'd never thought that lighting a candle would be the hardest part of magic. Large bursts of magic I could do with no problem, but it was the small things, the simple lighting of a candle, that I just seemed unable to manage. It was frustrating. I wanted to scratch my eyes out every time a big ball of fire escaped my hands and hit the wall behind the candle instead. Only a small flame, I just needed a small flame to light it and…

"You know," a strange voice said. It sounded like walking on gravel, rough and hard. I spun around, my familiar in front of me in an instant, protecting me from whoever stood in the door. "If you didn't put so much pressure on yourself, it would come naturally."

The ballerina was covering my face, blocking my view. I peered around her.

In the doorway to my bathroom stood a boy clad in black from head to toe. His hair was short but still managed to look tousled, and his eyes were the color of a bright afternoon sky. He leaned against the doorframe, arms crossed across his broad chest. His leather jacket was straining around his muscular arms. He was tall, much taller than Damien, and had the sort of face you'd expect to find in an underground pit fight. A scar cut over his left eye, as if someone had taken a razor and sliced all the way down from his temple to his jawline. The scar was stark against his golden skin and it made him look rugged and tough. I could see a tattoo snaking up the side of his neck. I couldn't see what it was, but the tips ended in ink blotches. He was a handsome man, I couldn't argue with that, but he was a handsome man standing in the doorway to my bathroom, uninvited and unmet.

"Who the hell are you?" I asked, gently pushing the ballerina out of my way to approach him. My hands became balls of fire and my nostrils flared. If the Dark Brotherhood had sent him to take me away, I was going to put up one hell of a fight. I didn't care how strong he was. I would make sure he remembered me for a long, long time. It didn't matter how strong he was, either—even the strongest of people were vulnerable to flames.

"Shhh, you'll wake everyone in the damned wing," he said, rolling his eyes. He had a slight accent—Scottish, maybe? It wasn't strong enough to distinguish, and I didn't care enough to listen more closely. He was an intruder. He had seen the ballerina. He was dangerous.

I had to know who he was, and I had to find out just how much he knew.

"Answer me," I hissed through gritted teeth. He threw his hands up in defeat, sighing.

"The name is Sebastian," he said, crossing one leg over the other as he leaned against the doorframe again. "I've come to ask for your help."

"My help?" I laughed. The ballerina came to sit on my shoulder, and he didn't seem to notice her at all. If he did, he didn't show any indication of it. He was calm and collected, as if a flaming ballerina was the most normal thing he had ever seen. It was like he was used to the idea. It was either that or he was too stupid to know what she was. The look in his eyes told me that he wasn't stupid at all. In fact, if a person could have intelligent eyes, he had them.

"The Dark Brotherhood knows about you. They are coming, and they are stronger than anything this world has ever known," he said nonchalantly. "They need to be stopped at all costs, and you are the only one who can help me do it."

"You're crazy," I accused, my heart hammering in my throat. The Dark Brotherhood… he knew about them and they knew about me. Assuming anything this man said could be trusted.

I didn't like the doubt that crept into my thoughts, the doubt that *he* had placed in my head. If he could find me, sneak up on me so easily, the Dark Brotherhood wasn't far behind. They could be here at any second. Unless he was part of the Dark Brotherhood and he was trying to trick me. There were too many possibilities and I started to feel a little lightheaded.

"Get out of here," I snapped, "before I—"

"Before you what, hmm? Before you turn me to dust? Before you call for help?" His grin was infuriating. How was he so sure of himself? How was he so certain that I wouldn't melt his bones right here and now? There was no way for him to know, unless he had something I wanted or needed. "I can assure you that none of those options will be beneficial to you."

"And why is that?" I retorted. If he had information, it would be more than the headmistress could have come up with. If I could find out what he knew, we'd certainly have more than we had a week ago. I had to humor him, and I had to milk him for as many details as I could.

"I have information about the Dark Brotherhood that no one else can give you. I have information on your family."

My heart seemed to stop, and the world went quiet. The owls stopped hooting; the crickets stopped their recitals. In that moment, it was only me and the mention of my family, hanging in the air like a balloon just waiting to be popped.

"My family? I don't have a family," I lied to him. I did have a family, a long time ago. I had a family that I'd lost and had never managed to find again.

"You had one long ago, Cornelia." My name rolled off his tongue. "A mother and a sister. I can help you find them, or at least, help you find out what happened to them."

"Why should I trust you?" It wasn't the first question that popped into mind but it was the most logical thing to ask. What did he know? Where were they? Did they remember me? Did they look for me? Had they abandoned me all those years ago? Did they hope I never found them again? There was list after list filled with questions.

"Why should *I* trust *you*?" He raised an eyebrow. I didn't have an answer for him. "We have a common enemy, and we are the only ones that can stop them. Your headmistress can't begin to comprehend how much power the Dark Brotherhood has, and I am sure that she thinks she isn't underestimating them. She is scared, and rightfully so. Everyone in this world should be afraid. They should be very, very afraid."

"And what are we supposed to do against power that no one else can stop? We're only two people, and to be honest with you, I can't even sense your magic." It had been bothering me since he'd introduced himself. He didn't have a magical presence. There was no sweetness in the air, save for my own. He didn't have magic; he was human. What could he possibly bring to the table?

"That's because I am hiding it from you," he said, shrugging.

"Why?"

"It seems you are not very fond of fire."

I wasn't sure what that was supposed to mean. "What?" I asked, my face contorted with confusion. "What is that supposed to mean?"

He sighed, rubbing his eyes with two fingers as if he was losing patience. Good, so was I. "Promise me that you won't do something stupid? Promise me that you won't freak out and make me chase after you, because I will catch up with you and then we are going to have a problem."

"I won't," I said, curious but also a little afraid.

"Promise me," he repeated.

"I promise."

He nodded, then looked back into my bedroom, toward my window. Was that how he had gotten in? Was that how he got into the academy without anyone noticing?

"Aodh," he said simply, his voice clear and commanding. The ballerina stiffened when he called out the word. She looked at me, wide-eyed, before forcing herself to look at the door again. When I joined her, I gasped and stumbled backward.

The full force of his magical aura crashed into me, taking my breath away. I doubled over. It sucked the air from the room and made my ears sing. I'd never felt anything like that before in my life. When I regained my balance, I looked through watery eyes to see what was on his shoulder. Aodh wasn't a word at all; it was a name.

It was the name of a flaming phoenix that now sat on his shoulder.

It was the name of his familiar.

CHAPTER 15:

NOT AS IT SEEMS

"I want to help," was the only thing I said as I barged into the headmistress' office.

She tilted her head to one side, setting down her pen on the desk, followed by her reading classes.

"I thought I told you to stay out of sight," she said, evenly and calmly. It was the worst tone of voice she could have used, to be perfectly honest. It was the voice she used when she was irritated, annoyed, fed up with whatever was going on around her. It was the voice she used when I'd screwed up and she was angry that she didn't have more control over me. Yes, the headmistress was a control freak, and I was the one person that no one, not even I, could control. It made for very, very good arguments.

"And I did," I said, nodding. "And you didn't come up with any information so far. Well, information found me, and it's much worse than we initially thought. It is much, much worse."

"And where exactly did you get this information?" she asked, knotting her fingers together. Her usual smile was replaced with the tight line she pressed her lips into. It was unsettling.

I tried to recall anything the boy said to suggest I couldn't tell the headmistress, but came up empty-handed. Still, I didn't want to tell her anything that would break his trust in me. I needed his information. I hadn't realized just how badly I wanted to find my family, or even find out what happened to them. My past was a mystery to me, and I'd locked it far away. That strange boy was the one thing I needed to unlock it.

He also possessed the exact same magic I did. There were so many things that I needed answers to. He could tell me things about my magic, about familiars. He could help me control it like he controlled his own power. There were so many possibilities with this boy, so many ways he could help me. I couldn't mess that up. I couldn't mess up my only opportunity to get answers. But he hadn't said anything about not telling people about him, so I told her.

"There was a boy in my room last night; he came out of nowhere," I began. "He said that there was a storm coming and that he needed me to fight it with him. That he needed the school's help to fight it. He said the Dark Brotherhood already knows about me, and that they are on their way to come and get me. They don't want me for my magic, they want me because I can stop them."

"There was a strange boy in your room, and you're only coming to me now? Lia, what were you thinking?" She got up from her chair. There was a cringing screech, and I winced. I was about to get a stern talking-to. If luck was on my side, I might just leave with my life. "What makes you think you can trust this boy?"

"I have a feeling," I admitted. It sounded much more stupid when I said it out loud than it had sounded in my head.

It was hard to explain. I just had a feeling about him. I knew that I could trust him with my life. I didn't know why or how. I didn't know how he had gotten me to calm down so fast and listen to him, either. He seemed too honest, too forthcoming to be a liar. I knew what liars looked like, and he wasn't one. Besides, he had a familiar… a flame familiar, just like I did. He was like me. He was exactly like me.

I bit my lip. I knew that my reasons for trusting him were flimsy at best, but it was the best thing we'd come up with so far. We had no other leads, no more information. I had no choice but to trust him. "There's one more thing."

The headmistress sighed. "What is it?"

"He has fire magic, just like me." I was quiet for a moment. The headmistress didn't say a single word, and I took it as a sign to go on. "And he has a familiar, too."

"Wait, what?" The headmistress came around her table to stand in front of me, her hands on my shoulders. Her touch wasn't as gentle as it usually was. "What did you say his name was?"

"Sebastian," I answered, moving to take a step back, but her hands were firm on my shoulders. Her nails lightly dug into my flesh.

"You stupid, stupid girl," she said, shaking me slightly. Her eyes were wide with panic.

I yanked my shoulders free, rubbing them as I looked at her. I'd never seen her like this. She seemed panicked and overwhelmed. Still, her insult didn't sit well with me. "Excuse me?"

"That is Olaf's son," she whispered, a hand on her forehead. She started pacing the room. "He's the heir to the Dark Brotherhood throne!"

"What?" It felt as if the rug was pulled from under my feet. "No! He said he wanted to take down the Dark Brotherhood. He said that—"

"The Abernathy men say a lot of things, Cornelia. What they say and what they do are two different things—they are two completely different things. They've found you. They know about you."

Her pacing was making me anxious, and my mouth had gone dry. Stupid… I was so, so stupid.

"What do we do now?" I asked, my voice shaking. I was an idiot. I was a damned idiot. The first sign of someone being like me and I'd lost all of my senses. The first sign of someone understanding me, and it was as if a blindfold had been tied over my eyes. Anyone could trick me into believing anything if they showed me what I wanted to see. They gave me what I wanted, only to take it all away when I least expected it. I had been certain he could be trusted. I had been so, so certain. How could I have been so stupid?

She turned to me again, and it was as if a lightbulb had flickered to life in her head. "If he comes around again, you pretend not to know who he is. You tell him that you will help, and you tell him that the school will help him, too. You get close to him; you try and find out as much as you possibly can." The plan was a bit insane, but it seemed better than mine: believe the first person that came along and let him lead me to my doom.

"He's not going to tell me anything if he's really out to get me."

"Lies are better than nothing." Her pacing stopped and she went back to her desk, sat down, and put her reading glasses back on. It was as if nothing had happened. "He's bound to mess up, and when he does, you will be there, listening intently."

"All this sounds a little dodgy to me," I mumbled. She picked up her pen and set it down again.

"He was right about one thing, Cornelia. You truly are the only person that can stop the Dark Brotherhood if they actually rise to power. You are the only one with enough raw magic to take them on. If that boy has even half the power you do, none of us stand a chance."

"Okay," I said, nodding. I wasn't going to go against her again. Look where that had gotten me.

"You can get back to class. If they already know about your existence, there's no use in hiding anymore. This might just be enough to get their attention and lure them into a trap." It made sense. Let them think that we suspected nothing; let them think we were being careless. If they came, we'd be ready for them. And although the chances of us beating them were slim, having the element of surprise was better than nothing.

I nodded, then turned to walk away. "Have the familiar with you at all times," she added. The ballerina's head shot up and she got to her feet, holding onto my hair as she turned on my shoulder to face the headmistress. This was the first time the ballerina had reacted to anything the headmistress or I said. "She will protect you, if anything were to happen."

"With my life," the ballerina vowed.

I stopped when I reached the door, turning around before I addressed what was bothering me. "You knew who Sebastian was. You knew when I mentioned that he had fire magic. You told me that I was the only one of my kind when clearly, there was another out there. Another with the same extent of magic I have, one that has a familiar. You knew all of this. Why did you tell me that I was alone?"

"It was easier to tell you that you were alone than to tell you there was someone else like you out there, but he was the one destined to ruin the Earth as we know it. How do you tell a child that the one thing she is so terribly afraid of might be the thing that kills everything she has known? How do you tell a sweet little girl that she has a direct opposite—a wild and unruly boy with a mirror image of her magic?"

"That's easy," I said, tears stinging my eyes. "You tell the kid that she is not alone, that there is someone else out there that has the same fire. You tell her that there is a boy that she should never trust, never get mixed up with. You tell her the truth. Maybe, if you had, that little girl wouldn't have possibly gotten herself and everyone around her killed."

CHAPTER 16:

SORE THUMB

If I thought I stood out like a sore thumb before, I had another think coming.

I'd been walking back and forth in front of the big doors that led to the dining hall, contemplating my options back to front and front to back. I had to go in regardless. Every option I had included me going to dinner tonight, and back to school tomorrow. My excuse would be that I had been terribly sick, and the notes from the headmistress would confirm this. However, there was one little problem—in the shape of a ballerina on my shoulder.

I couldn't lie, I was nervous. I knew they would find out about her eventually. I couldn't leave her in my room every day until I was done with classes. It wasn't that I didn't trust her, but I didn't trust myself without her. I didn't want to feel that hollowness in my stomach ever again. I couldn't be separated from her. So, they would find out no matter what, but did I announce her existence tonight in front of the whole academy, or did I wait and take it one class at a time?

I realized that I wanted to announce her. I wanted everyone to know she existed. I wanted to show her off. Not only because of the trap we were trying to set, but because I was sick of hiding. I was sick of hiding who I was. I hadn't realized it until then. I'd always wanted to be normal, always wanted to blend in, but now that I had the chance to, I didn't want it. Getting my familiar gave me a new sort of confidence that I didn't think I could ever have possessed.

It was strange, too strange to explain. In just one week, my entire life had been flipped on its side. Everything I thought I knew, everything I thought I was, was wrong. I was not some out-of-control witch who wasn't skilled enough to control her own power. No, I was an elemental with the power of summoning, of creating a familiar—a familiar with a personality, a voice, a spirit. The spirit of my magic.

This familiar was my magic. All my life, I had been ashamed of it. I'd tried to tell myself that I was afraid of it, but that wasn't the case. I was ashamed. I was ashamed of my lack of control. The flames have never been what really scared me. The fire has always just been a part of me, trying to protect itself. But I wasn't ashamed anymore. I had done something none of them could dream of. I'd done it the first time I tried. I wanted them to see it. I wanted to see their faces as they saw the flame on my shoulder.

But then again... What would they think? Wouldn't it just cast me out even more? Was this even permitted in the academy? We weren't allowed to play with magic outside of the classroom, but did this count? The headmistress knew about me practicing with Mr. Henry. That wouldn't have been a problem. She'd told me to do this. But the rest of the school? My friends? I didn't know how they would react. Were they going to be scared of me? What was worse: them thinking I was a coward, or them being afraid of me?

Wendy's voice rang in my head, louder than it was when she actually spoke to me. It was time for me to man up. I was sick of being the outcast, sick of being the one everyone pushed away. I was the person everyone read about. My magic was what myths were made of. My magic—not theirs, not anyone else's. I deserved to let it show.

In a way, this was me showing the Dark Brotherhood that I wasn't afraid of them. That they could come for me and I wouldn't care. It wasn't true, of course, but it felt good to think about it like that. It felt good to imagine myself as a hero, as someone who wasn't afraid. I wanted to be that person, and pretending to be that person was the first step to becoming her. Perhaps, if I pretended enough, I would convince myself that I wasn't afraid.

"What are you waiting for?" the ballerina asked, crossing her arms.

"I'm thinking," I said.

"What's there to think about? You have a familiar, they don't. You have the power of the sun, they don't. It's just how it is." She shrugged.

"I've always been more of a hider than a shower."

"What do you think witches do at an academy, Lia? They learn. They become stronger. They *want* to become stronger. They want to be the strongest." She opened the palm of her hand and a little version of herself stood there, like an action figure. "You already are the strongest. Don't hide it. Everyone wants to be you."

I grinned at her. "When did you become so wise?"

"It's all the teenage dramas we've been watching," she groaned, and I chuckled.

With my newfound confidence and a very proud-looking ballerina on my shoulder, I pushed the doors open and walked toward our table as if nothing was different. I had texted Wendy earlier to grab an extra plate of food for me. In some way, I'd thought that going straight to the table would be better than standing in line to get my dinner. If I went to the table, I wouldn't be alone for longer than was necessary. If I went straight to the table, my friends wouldn't have the opportunity to realize what was going on and leave. Even with the confidence that the ballerina gave me, I needed the comfort of knowing that my friends were there. Even if only for a few seconds.

The room fell silent. There were no whispers, no muffled laughter. No, the room was quiet. The only sounds were my boots on the floor and the flickering flames on my shoulder. I could have sworn the ballerina grew brighter. The little minx wanted to make an impact. She *wanted* people to see her. I fought a smile. It worked. I didn't look at anyone and for a moment, I nearly thought that I was alone in the dining hall. But I wasn't, because I saw my friends, grinning like bloody Cheshire cats. They were smiling. Not running, not whispering. They were grinning, as if I had finally done something they'd all known I would do eventually.

I took my usual seat, bidding everyone a good evening before I examined the food in front of me. Beef stew on rice. It wasn't macaroni, but it was better than nothing. I dug in and when I noticed none of them were talking, I lifted my head. "What?"

"You have something on your shoulder," Patrick pointed out, examining the ballerina. She sat perfectly still, the complete opposite of the gymnastics that were taking place in my stomach. I couldn't decide if it was excitement or nerves. Either way, it was there, and it wasn't going away anytime soon.

"Indeed, there is." I nodded, taking another bite of my food. I feigned nonchalance when, in reality, I was dying to know what they thought. I was dying to know what they would say if they knew anything about what I had learned about my magic—about the volcanos, the role of the familiar, the darkness that was coming.

"Um," Nina said, her eyebrows creasing, "is that what everyone has been talking about?"

"The demon I talk to?" I asked. The stew was better than normal. I had to find out who was on duty tonight. It was better than anything Cook Magna made. Nina nodded. "If you want to call a familiar a demon, sure."

Patrick burst out laughing, shaking his head as he reached out toward Nina, Wendy, and Damien. "Pay up. I told you it was real."

"You said the demon was real," Damien said, narrowing his eyes at Patrick. "This isn't a demon. Besides, I knew about her. Why would I bet against myself? The demon doesn't exist, which means you owe us, man."

"You knew? That's not fair!" Patrick exclaimed, glaring at Damien. Then, he looked at me. "How long has this brother known?"

I opened my mouth to answer but Damien responded before I could. "Like, a week."

"That's not fair, bro."

"Hey." Damien grinned, his hands behind his head. "I don't make the rules, man. We never said we couldn't bet on things we knew."

"You guys bet on me?" I raised an eyebrow.

"We always do," Wendy admitted, gnawing on a piece of beef.

"Are we all just going to ignore the fact that there is a familiar on her shoulder? An actual familiar?" Nina came a little closer to the ballerina, examining every inch of her. The ballerina seemed to enjoy the attention. "How is this possible?"

"It's Lia, Nina. Anything is possible with her," Damien said, winking at me. I rolled my eyes and shrugged. This was not the appropriate time for this.

Now that I was back and the secret was out, Damien would want to talk to me, and I wasn't sure I was ready for that just yet. He'd want to talk about everything that had happened, about us. Perhaps, if I ignored his flirtations, he wouldn't be so eager. Perhaps it would put him off for a bit. I hoped with everything within me that it would work. I didn't know how else I could possibly tell him that I didn't think now was the right time for us. That I didn't feel that way about him, but that I didn't have the time to figure out how I actually *did* feel.

"Mr. Henry helped me create her. I don't know how I did it myself, but I did and here we are." I took the chance to glance around quickly. "All eyes on me." The room was still quiet, staring at me. Sometimes, I could hear the scratching of a fork, but that was it.

"When I told you to man up, Lia, I didn't think you would go and summon a familiar," Wendy said, a small smile on her face. "Trust you to walk the extra mile."

"Mr. Henry thought it was a good idea to get to know my magic. You know? Find out why it acts the way it does." I didn't know why I was explaining this to them. It wasn't as if they would understand any of it. They didn't have the problems I did with their magic. Their magic obeyed their every beck and call. They never understood why I didn't have that ability, and they probably never would. Still, I felt the need to try. Even if it was just to make conversation.

"I've heard stories about familiars. About their devoted loyalty to their masters. I heard that they would pillage entire villages for their masters and bring home gold and riches," she said. I'd heard the story she was telling me about, and it was utter garbage. "I can understand you wanting one. They are badass. But what I don't understand is, in your reasoning, how are you going to get to know it if it can't talk?" Nina asked.

Suddenly, the ballerina turned her head to Nina, who yelped and scooted away from me. Wendy was holding her in her arms, looking wide-eyed at the ballerina, who smiled at them both.

"But I *can* talk," she said, hopping off my shoulder and landing gracefully on the table.

Her little feet hardly made a sound on the plywood. Wherever she stepped, little embers flew into the sky. This was an effect I had never seen her use before. She was being dramatic. I wanted to whack her, to tell her not to attract even more attention.

"I can understand your confusion," she continued, twirling like a real ballerina. "But my master is no ordinary witch, and I am no ordinary magic."

The ballerina caused quite the stir and soon enough, a crowd surrounded our table. It was out of sorts. The kids at the academy typically never marveled at magic—it was something they were used to, something that they too possessed. The ballerina seemed to handle herself just fine, singeing fingers that came just a little too close to her.

"Now that the secret is out," Damien whispered in my ear, leaning closer to me so only I could hear him as the rest of the students were distracted by the ballerina, "I think it's time we talked."

In that instant, the ballerina looked at me, her eyes growing wide and her head shaking ever so slightly. It was hardly noticeable. Then, there was skin against my hand: another hand. Only then did I realize what the ballerina was trying to tell me. I had to get away from him if I was going to avoid it.

Before he could entwine our fingers, I reached out my hand to pick up the ballerina. I hoped that Damien thought it was coincidence. I hoped he thought that I was merely trying to protect my familiar from prodding fingers. From the corner of my eye, I could see his hand pulling away, balling into a fist.

The ballerina didn't stop glaring at him the rest of the evening.

CHAPTER 17:

MR. HENRY AND ME

"I want you to toss a fireball at me."

"You want me to do what?" I asked, not sure I'd heard Mr. Henry correctly.

"You heard me, Lia," he said. "I want you to throw a fireball at me."

"Do you have a death wish?"

He chuckled. "It's easy to lose control if there isn't anything at risk. My life is at risk now. So, get a small fireball in your hand and throw it at me. I will catch it with water, if it's small enough."

"If?" I looked over at him dubiously.

"Okay, listen, you can't be scared of the fire forever. You are strong, and you have a familiar that you should have grown closer to by now. You know your magic. She is your magic," he explained. "The wildness that you have always felt inside of you was that ballerina on your shoulder. It was her, trying to get out to protect you. It was her that was trying to protect herself from you trying to leash her. Now that she's out, she can protect you. Now that you know her, you know how to handle her. You know what makes her tick. You know how to calm her down. Now, get that fireball and throw it at me."

"I will not be held responsible if your hair catches on fire," I said, cringing at what I was about to do.

The ballerina leaned closer to me, whispering in my ear. "There's so much product in his hair, I am surprised he can walk past a candle without being set on fire."

"I heard that," Mr. Henry said, but it didn't stop my giggle.

I knew what they were trying to do. They were trying to get me to relax, to let my magic do its thing. It was like a caged dog, my magic. When it was in its cage, it would go crazy, biting and barking. But once it was let out, it was calmer. It was the sort of dog that rested its head on your lap while watching television, begging you for treats. It was the sort of dog that brought you your newspaper.

I had to relax and let my magic out of its cage. I had to shake off the shackles and embrace it. I had to treat the flames to fresh air and some exercise.

My fingertips tingled as they sparked, igniting a flame no bigger than the palm of my hand. It was hot, but not hot enough to burn me. Instead, this flame was comforting. It was nice. I smiled as I looked at it, watching as it stayed the exact same size. It didn't grow or flicker. This was a perfectly still flame.

I put one hand over the other, pressing the flame into a tight ball. It reminded me of rolling a snowball. When I was finished, I looked at Mr. Henry who had his feet planted a comfortable width apart, waiting to catch my fireball as if we were playing catch.

I took a deep breath, reminding myself that the ballerina was here, my familiar was here. Everything was going to be fine. There was nothing to be afraid of. Everything was utterly and completely fine.

Finally, I threw the fireball at Mr. Henry, and it moved too fast for my eyes to follow. All I saw was an orange and red stripe that led from me to my teacher.

Mr. Henry had cat-like reflexes and caught the fireball with a hand wrapped in water. The water did not put out the fire; instead, it cradled the ball of fire perfectly, protecting it from the assault of wind.

Mr. Henry grinned at me. "What did I tell you, kid?"

"He's never going to let you hear the end of this," the ballerina mumbled, playing with stray locks of my hair.

"Now, catch it again. Don't question it," he instructed. "Just let your body react naturally."

I didn't have time to think, didn't have time to consider my options. My body moved on its own, stretching out to catch the ball of fire. It connected with my hand, still hot but not blistering. I stared at it for a bit, amazed by the control.

No, not control. I wasn't controlling the magic. That was a thought I had to get out of my head.

There was no controlling the magic, I knew that now. I was not controlling it, but rather telling it what to do. The magic itself controlled the form it took, the heat it emitted. It knew exactly how hot it had to be, how big it had to be to stay under control. All this time, I thought that I had to think about my magic like other sorcerers thought about theirs. But my magic was nothing like theirs. My magic had a mind of its own; it had intelligence. And it needed that intelligence to avoid being misused. It needed to know what to do because it was impossible for its caster to know themselves. The volcanos inside of me scared the hell out of me at first, but now I understood. I understood that I had the power to call on that magic, but I did not have the power to control it. I could guide it, yes, but I shouldn't interfere.

"You're starting to understand now," the ballerina said with a giant grin on her face. "No one ever explained it to me like this."

"That's because no one understood your magic."

I looked at Mr. Henry, who was waiting for me to toss the ball back to him. No one except for him, it would seem. How did he have such a wealth of knowledge about my magic? My magic was nothing like his. He didn't have a familiar, he'd never come in contact with anyone else that controls fire. I shook my head. He was the only one who was actually helping me. I didn't care where he got his information from; all I cared about was that he was sharing it with me.

"I want to try something different," I said.

Mr. Henry raised his eyebrows. "I thought I was in charge here."

"I don't know what gave you that idea," I teased, then stepped back. "I want you to send water my way."

"Excuse me?" he mimicked my confusion that I'd had at the beginning of this lesson.

I told him my idea, what I wanted to try. He didn't seem very impressed with me, but I made him agree to it, nonetheless. If

I was going to get better at my magic, I had to be able to handle anything that came my way. I had to be able to handle anything that could snuff out my flames.

I would start with water and work my way up. We'd start out slow, small. And then, we could make the waves bigger. I had to learn how to counter other magics. Especially if they were as efficient at putting out my flames like Mr. Henry's water.

We got ready.

I stood in the middle of the clearing, making sure that there were no trees close by. Mr. Henry stood at the border of the forest and the meadow. "Are you sure you want me to do this?"

"I'm sure," I confirmed, then looked at the ballerina. She was grinning at me.

I watched as Mr. Henry summoned a wave as tall as he was. The water was a beautiful blue; it seemed almost animated.

The wave came closer, closer, and my heart beat faster. I really hoped I could do this.

I heard the wave before it crashed into me, sizzling away into nothingness. There was a steam cloud around me, and my body was coated in flames. His magic had no effect on me in this form. When it got close, it merely evaporated. I huffed, disappointed.

"Is that the best you can do?" I asked, the flames around me turning into smoke, then disappearing.

"All right, Cornelia. You've proven that you can defend yourself," he said, something different in his voice now. It was a little strained, a little forced. Perhaps he was annoyed that he couldn't put out the fire just now. It must have been that? But it looked as if he was thinking, worrying?

"I am going to summon a pool of water now, and you are going to shoot a ball of fire into it," he commanded. "Don't make it hot. I want to see how long your flame can last under the circumstances. Sometimes, you won't be able to use the heat to that extent, and then you're screwed."

"So, you want to see if my fire can last when it's submerged in water?"

He nodded. That was ridiculous. Of course, the fire wasn't going to last in the water. What was he thinking? Still, I didn't argue with him. I decided to humor him, instead.

It took only a few seconds for a body of water to form in front of us. It nearly seemed as if it was in a glass tank, only there was no tank at all. Mr. Henry was keeping it still as a pool of water. I looked at him. It was as if he didn't even notice the effort.

I did what he told me to, then. I formed a ball of fire in my hand and tossed it into the water, but it died out as soon as it hit the cool blue surface. I sighed with disappointment, looking at the ballerina who merely shrugged and floated away to the tree line. As if suggesting I was on my own. She found herself a nice spot in the shade and lied down.

"Try that again, Cornelia, but focus on keeping it alive this time. Don't just throw it, keep it alive." Mr. Henry still looked too anxious for my liking, and it made me uneasy.

I rolled my shoulders, closed my eyes, and formed the ball in my hand once again, imagining that it had a protective layer around it. I tossed it at the water, but we got the same results.

Mr. Henry seemed to breathe a sigh of relief and it snapped something inside my chest.

My eyes felt as if they were made from fire, and from my hands shot a fireball straight toward the pool of water. Flames rose in my throat and my fingers twitched, focusing all my energy into keeping the blaze alive underwater. There was just something that I found very satisfying about proving people wrong, about knocking the smirk off someone's face completely. I didn't know why Mr. Henry's reaction triggered me, but I was grateful that it did. He looked at me, mouth agape. Smiling at him, I decided to rub salt in the wound.

I molded the fireball inside of the tank, shaping it until it was a baby dolphin. I made it swim through the water, a flaming fish. It moved gracefully, just like I'd told it to with my hands and then, with one mighty leap, it jumped out of the water. It burned brighter than the sun and Mr. Henry had to cover his eyes. The light was blinding, brighter than I ever thought my flames could burn.

The dolphin crashed into the water again, splashing as it swam all the way down to the bottom, only to turn around and swim upward again, gathering speed for yet another lump. I laughed heartily when it emerged again. It was the strangest thing I had ever seen in my entire life—a fish made of flames, swimming through water. Flames existing underwater. I never knew it was possible. I never knew that I was capable of doing such things.

"Remarkable," Mr. Henry breathed, walking toward the tank. The dolphin splashed him once, causing a string of curses to leave his mouth, before popping its head from the side of the invisible tank. Gingerly, Mr. Henry reached out to touch the dolphin. He didn't recoil, didn't flinch. He huffed a breath of air that could have been a chuckle. "Shit."

CHAPTER 18:

Awful Teachers

Apart from the stares that had followed me around since my grand appearance at dinner the previous week, things had gone pretty smoothly. There were no incidents with Margot, even though I was certain that she was going to make trouble sooner or later. She was not the sort of girl who just let things slide. She was out for Damien and me both now, and when she did attack, I was ready for her. Yes, this time I was going to fight back. I was done being walked over. How did I expect to beat the Dark Brotherhood if I couldn't even stand up and face my high school bully? No, that was out of the question. There would be no more bullying from her. Especially not when it involved me or my friends. She had another think coming if she thought she could come after me again. She'd done it one too many times.

But Margot still hadn't made her big appearance, and I was starting to settle into a routine. School was school and I tried to avoid Damien as much as possible. I had the excuse of having to catch up on the classes I'd missed when I was in the tower, but the excuse was only going to last so long. At least at dinner, breakfast, and lunch, the other three were with us. He wouldn't talk about what happened in front of them. At least, I was hoping he wouldn't. After school, I had a three-hour practice session with Mr. Henry and then it was time for dinner before I headed up to my room, drowning in research, projects, and homework until I passed out from exhaustion.

The ballerina still hadn't told me her name, but that was fine. She'd slowly begun to crawl her fiery little way into my heart, and I couldn't imagine my days without her. She was a mischievous little rascal, and she enjoyed annoying Wendy most of all. To Wendy's credit, she never got angry at the ballerina. Instead, she'd made a special bed in her backpack for her to sleep in when the class was particularly boring. The ballerina liked my friends, all except Damien. She said that she had an off feeling about him, but I shrugged it off. She probably felt my reluctance to be alone with him through our bond and took it as something else.

But all in all, things were going well.

It was unsettling. I was afraid of letting my guard down. I was afraid that, whenever I allowed myself to relax, Sebastian would work his way into my room again and turn my whole world upside down. We had scheduled to meet that night, exactly a week after he had last been in contact with me. I still wasn't sure what was going to happen or what I was going to say to him. I wasn't sure if he'd even show up. Perhaps he had somehow found out about what I told the headmistress. Perhaps he knew that I knew who exactly he was and why he was contacting me. Those were a lot of "Perhapses" and not enough "For certains." I didn't like it one bit. That boy was a mystery to me that I just couldn't uncover.

I found myself dreaming about him in classes—the way his eyes danced when he smirked, the way he spoke to his familiar as if they were old buddies. I understood that bond now. It only took the creation of the familiar to form that bond, and it only grew stronger as time progressed. I daydreamed about that smirk and how good he was at camouflaging the truth. He hasn't made any effort to contact me again, and perhaps that was for the best. I couldn't stand the thought of him brainwashing me with more lies. He was the son of the man who wanted me dead. He was a spy, a filthy spy, and I had to go along with it if he ever came back. I had to pretend like there was nothing wrong, and I didn't know how I was going to manage it. I was a terrible liar. I hoped he never showed his face again.

"Who can tell me how the bond between caster and magic works?" Mr. Henry's voice brought me back to the present. I was vaguely aware of my chewed pen as I pulled it from my mouth. What the hell was he even talking about?

Margot was the only one who put her hand up. In typical Mr. Henry fashion, he sighed and nodded for her to answer. It was apparent that he didn't like her very much, either, and it made for good entertainment in class. She didn't seem to notice, though. In her mind, everyone liked her.

"I like to think of the magic as a servant. It has to do what we want it to," she said, popping a chewing gum bubble nearly the size of her head.

Mr. Henry contemplated her answer. "It's different for every person. Who else wants to take a shot?"

To everyone's surprise, Wendy put up her hand. "If it's different for everyone, why are we even discussing this? I mean, wouldn't it be more beneficial if we learned how to actually use it? Aren't you the one who is supposed to teach us these things?"

A note dropped onto my desk, neatly folded with my name scribbled on the front. It was Damien's handwriting. I looked over at him, where he sat at the front of the class. He was looking at me, his eyes searching my face for something. I wasn't sure what he was looking for, but I knew he wasn't going to find whatever it was.

Opening the note, I found nine words. Nine words that made my stomach drop.

"You look pretty, as always. When can we talk?" I looked back up at him, then shook my head. I needed him to stop. I needed him to back off for a bit. If only for a little while.

Mr. Henry chuckled at Wendy's answer, catching me off guard. I broke eye contact with Damien to look at Mr. Henry. "I'm asking you this because I want to understand how everyone sees their magic. Once you understand your magic, you will have more control over it." He then turned to me, smiling. I wanted to melt into the chair. "Miss Strange, what's your bond with your magic?"

I shook my head, silently begging him to pick someone else, but he just nodded persistently. I sighed. "Magic isn't a servant, it's an extension of oneself. You have to get to know it before you can manipulate it." I turned my head toward Margot, addressing her directly. "It's not something you control. It doesn't belong to you. It *is* you."

Margot laughed and rolled her eyes. "Is that why you have *so* much control over your magic?" The jab hit me hard, but I pretended as if I didn't hear her.

"Interesting," Mr. Henry said, obviously amused by the fact that I'd used his own words to explain my magic to him. He was about to open his mouth when the door to his classroom opened and a seething Mrs. Finnick came rushing in. Her face was red with anger. "Glenda, what can I—"

"Where is she?" Her voice seemed higher than it usually was. She turned to face the classroom, then her eyes locked on me. I felt like a zebra who'd suddenly come face to face with a crocodile. There was nowhere to run from its deadly maw, no way to escape death.

I'd never felt true terror more than in that moment. She marched toward me, every footstep angry and audible. It almost sounded as if she were walking in a cartoon. It sure looked like it.

"You little witch," she accused, waving her finger in my face. I swallowed. "I know it was you."

"Me?" I asked, my voice a little cracked. "What is it that you think I did, Mrs. Finnick?"

"Glenda," Mr. Henry intervened, interrupting her as she was about to say something else. "This is highly unprofessional. Whatever happened, I am sure there is a logical explanation for it."

I smiled weakly at Mr. Henry, a silent thanks.

Mrs. Finnick's eye twitched. "This girl set the entire greenhouse on fire. There's nothing but ashes left!"

Anger took over every other emotion I felt. It was one thing to accuse me of something that I could have possibly done, but this? How stupid did she think I was?

"You think I did that?" I got to my feet. I didn't know whether I should be mortified or insulted, and settled somewhere in between. "There's a whole academy full of students. How does it being a fire prove that it was me? I don't just go around snapping my fingers, setting greenhouses on fire for sport, Mrs. Finnick."

"You are the only one with that sort of magic, girl," she hissed, disgusted.

"Glenda." Mr. Henry was walking toward us now.

Mrs. Finnick didn't pay any attention to him; instead, she was fully invested in staring me down. I didn't back down. There was no way that I was going to admit to something I hadn't done. It could have been anyone, it could have been an accident.

"Yes, and there are no matches in the entire school," I countered, feeling my nostrils flaring. The ballerina was now on my shoulder again, her arms crossed.

"Are you suggesting that I'm lying?" she demanded.

I shrugged. "I'm not suggesting anything. Not like you, blatantly accusing me of something without having your facts straight."

"And who do you suggest it was, hm?"

"There's a whole academy that wants to see my head on a stake," I said. "Take your pick, Mrs. Finnick."

"Are you just going to let her talk to me like this?" She turned to Mr. Henry, who merely shrugged.

"To be perfectly honest, I probably would have said something much worse if I were in her shoes. I'll ask around and see if anyone saw anything suspicious, but I can assure you that it was not Miss Strange. She isn't stupid enough to leave her signature after doing something like that. Either someone is trying to frame her, or it was merely a prank that has gone too far. Either way, I would like you to leave my classroom now so I can continue with my lesson."

Mrs. Finnick gave me one last glare, huffing before she marched out of the classroom. I sighed with relief. "Thank you," was all I managed to say.

Mr. Henry patted me on the shoulder. "We'll discuss this later. Take a seat. We're not done with today's lesson yet."

All eyes were on me now, Margot grinning like a cat who ate a canary. I felt my fire rise in my chest. A small hand tugging at my hair was the only thing that kept me from leaping out of my chair and attacking her. I was certain it was her, certain she was trying to get me into trouble. I wouldn't put it past her. But, then again, she wasn't nearly clever enough to pull that off. She relied on brute force. She wasn't sneaky. At least, not this sneaky. It must have been someone else. It had to be someone who was trying to get me expelled—to get me alone—or it was just another high school prank. I was willing to bet on the former.

There was no chance that this was an accident. The more I thought about it, the more malicious the entire situation felt. How could it have been an accident? The smallest fire would have set off the sprinklers. No, this was someone who knew exactly what they were doing. Someone, perhaps, with the same magic as me. Someone who wanted to get my attention, to let me know what he was capable of.

Everything fell into place, then. It must have been Sebastian. I couldn't think of any other explanation.

The rest of Mr. Henry's class went by in a blur and when the bell rang for lunch, I decided to skip the rest of the day altogether. What use was school when I was probably being tracked at that very moment? I had to talk to Sebastian. I had to confront him and perhaps, if I was lucky, get some answers from him. I ignored every call of my name; I ignored the way the ballerina had to hold on to my hair as I made my way to my tower. I didn't have time to talk to anyone. I didn't have time to explain what I was going to do and why I had to do it. I fully intended to blow off my afternoon practice with Mr. Henry, as well. There were more pressing matters at hand.

The ballerina didn't say a word as I locked the tower door, opened the window that Sebastian had climbed through the last time he'd visited, and waited. I sat like that for hours, brooding, wallowing in self-pity. Things had been going so well. Things were going so bloody well, but it took only one act of malice to screw it all up. I wasn't going to stand for it. I was not going to let this boy ruin my life. I was going to confront him, to fight him if I had to. And then, I was going to fight anyone else that came my way with their whips and threats of death. I was not going to die. I'd been pushed around enough. I'd had enough to deal with concerning my magic alone. I had to sort this out before it piled up.

I wanted a normal life after all of this was over. And the first step toward that was sorting out this mess with the greenhouse.

CHAPTER 19:

A DATE WITH MISCHIEF

He was on the floor as soon as he planted both of his feet in my tower. I held him down, wearing gloves of flames on my hands. Sebastian swore colorfully. I heard another string of curses from behind me and turned to see the ballerina was holding down the phoenix, as well.

"What the hell are you doing?" he said, his own hands erupting in flames.

"Me?" I asked. "You're the one who set the damned greenhouse on fire, you maniac!"

"What the hell are you talking about?" he said, his brows furrowed in confusion. In a split second, my anger vanished and I realized what I was doing and where I was. I had waited hours for him to come, plotted everything I was going to do to him, and now… Now, I wasn't so sure of myself anymore. He wasn't fighting me—in fact, he was laying perfectly still beneath me. This caught me off-guard more than anything else.

"I know who you are, Sebastian. You thought you could just come in here, pretend to help me, and then hand me over to your father?" If my body wasn't burning hot, I probably would have cried. Not because I was sad or angry, but because I was so, so frustrated.

This seemed to have an impact on him and he flipped us around, pinning me to the floor instead. His grip was vise-like around my wrists and my nostrils flared. "I came to you for help, Cornelia. Not to hand you over. Damn, what kind of guy do you think I am?"

"The sort with an evil father," I spat. His face flashed with something that resembled hurt, but it vanished as soon as it appeared. "The heir to the Dark Brotherhood?"

"Fair enough," he said with a sigh. "I'll explain everything, I swear. But I have to let go of you first. Promise me that you won't try anything stupid?"

"I can't make any promises," I hissed, but it was enough for him.

He peeled himself off of me, then held out a hand to help me out. I refused it, shaking the dust from my pants.

"I want to see my father dead as much as the next guy. Perhaps even more." His voice was low, laced with something more than just hate. It was an emotion I'd never seen before, an emotion that I hadn't even believed existed. "I am not on his side, Cornelia. I came to you for a reason. If I wanted to hand you over to him, I would have done so the first night we met. I am not your enemy."

"Why would you want your own father dead?"

He pushed a hand through his hair, chewing on his bottom lip before turning to face me fully. "He killed my mother and little brother, okay? They wanted to run, to get away from him, and he shot them. They didn't deserve to die, but he does. I don't care how I have to do it."

"Why didn't you tell me this the other day?" I was a fool for asking that. He didn't owe me his sad story, then—hell, he didn't owe it to me now, either. It was personal and it was dark. And I was a stranger.

"Because I didn't think it really mattered," he admitted. "I want him dead. He wants you dead. I figured the enemy of my enemy is my friend, or whatever."

"That was stupid," I said, sighing. It was only then that I realized the ballerina was still trying to keep the phoenix down. I chuckled. "You can let him go now."

She almost looked disappointed, pointing two fingers at her own eyes before pointing them at the other familiar. It was very amusing seeing such a small creature saying she had an eye on a damned glorified bird.

"What happened to the greenhouse?" he asked, looking at the phoenix as it landed on his shoulder.

"Someone set it on fire," I said. Someone, not Sebastian. I had that feeling again, that feeling of trust. He could have been making everything up, but he could also be telling the truth. I chose to believe him. I had trusted my gut the first time, and for some reason, I trusted it again this time. "One of the professors thought it was me."

"And you thought I did it because?" He waited for me to finish his sentence. I sighed.

"Because it's the only logical explanation."

He nodded. "That, or someone was trying to prank you. Or

the Dark Brotherhood has someone at the school that is trying to alienate you from the rest of the academy. If they think you're dangerous, they will push you aside."

"I don't even know where to start looking for such a person," I said, plopping down on my bed. He shrugged.

"Maybe start with the person who hates you the most," he suggested. "If it isn't that person, it must be the Dark Brotherhood."

"I don't think it will be someone on the inside," I said, thinking back to try and remember a single suspicious person at the academy. "The headmistress is very particular about who she hires. She won't allow a spy into the academy."

"The thing about a good spy is that you don't know he's a spy." He was making good points. I hated it.

"Are you saying that there are Dark Brotherhood members in the academy? Could they be students?" Students would have been the logical answer. The teachers were voted for by the parents of the students, and they wouldn't vote in a teacher they didn't trust.

He shrugged. "It's possible. They have people everywhere. But no, I don't think it'll be a student. It's not my father's style to employ anyone below the age of 20. He says we're too soft, too easy to manipulate. I don't even know who his right-hand man is. He'd rather have older soldiers."

"So, if there were someone here," I began, pushing the list of students out of my head and instead bringing up one of the teachers. Still, I couldn't imagine any of them actually doing something like that. "It would have to be a teacher."

"Hey, that's a very far stretch. I know you have enemies here, and—"

"How do you know that?" I interrupted.

"You did your research on me, I did my research on you." He shrugged. He wasn't afraid to admit that he spied on me.

I nodded. "Fair enough."

"My point is that it could be one of them."

"I don't know." The idea that someone would have gone to those lengths to get to me was a bit hard to believe. Especially as a stupid prank. "Margot doesn't seem like the sort of person who would set a greenhouse on fire just to spite me."

"Margot?" Sebastian snorted. "Any person named Margot is bound to plot evil things."

I sighed. "Why are you even here?"

"I came to see you," he said, a look of confusion in his face. "I had to find out if you were in or not."

"I don't know," I shrugged, toeing the floor with my boot.

"You don't know?"

"That's what I said."

"Why?"

"Because how do I know I can trust you? My life is at risk, here. I can't just go around trusting every boy that slips into my bedroom through my window and tells me that he needs my help to kill his father."

There was a whole list of reasons why I shouldn't have trusted him, but I did. That wasn't the real reason why I wasn't sure. I didn't know, because an hour ago, I was still certain I was going to kill him with my bare hands. I was also afraid. I had tried not to be, but I was. If I agreed, everything would become a reality.

"Hey," he said, holding his hands up. "If you say it like that, you make me sound like some sort of creep."

"Aren't you?"

"Listen," he said with a chuckle, "I can't convince you that you can trust me. It's just something you are going to have to decide for yourself. I am not going to beg you for your help. You don't strike me as the type of girl who would take kindly to begging, and to be honest, I'm much too good-looking to beg. Yes, I need your help, but I will find another way to overthrow my father and take down his organization if you refuse. And if we don't work together, you're not going to stand a chance against my father and his men. That much I can guarantee you."

"So, if I help you, you'll help me?"

He nodded. "You scratch my back and I will scratch yours. In this case, if we kill him, it solves both our problems."

I turned to the ballerina, hoping to find the answer in her eyes. I didn't. I only found her staring at the phoenix. She didn't blink. I nudged her with a foot. "What do you think? Can we trust them?"

She shrugged. "I don't like them, but just because I don't like them doesn't mean we can't trust them. I don't sense anything that would make me think they were here to hurt us. Usually, we can sense danger but with them..." She trailed off, shrugging again. "Nothing. I sense more danger from that friend of yours than these two."

"Damien?" I laughed. She really didn't like him.

She nodded. "Besides, if they do betray us, we can turn them both to ash."

Sebastian laughed, then frowned and swallowed. "She's serious?"

"I am," she responded. I fought back a grin. The control he had over his magic was far more advanced than I had. I could sense it. I could sense the wildness in his magic. It was wild, but it wasn't restless. It was nothing like mine.

The phoenix narrowed his eyes at her, and she beamed. I still wasn't sure if he could talk, but he did have a personality. Which meant he must have been like the ballerina. And he had a name. If Sebastien knew the name of his familiar, he was a few steps ahead of me. I hoped it was just a name he made up.

"Fine," I said, "I'll team up with you. But no more secrets, and no more digging around in my business. I also expect all the information on my family."

"After," he agreed, then held out a hand coated in flames.

My flames instantly coated my own hand and I reached out, shaking his. Our magic mingled, dancing around our hands like old friends, finally reunited.

"Also," he said, shuddering when we released each other's hands, "let go of that damned magic of yours. It gives me anxiety."

"What?"

"You know," he said, waving his hands in the air, "let it loose. It should be free, like waves. You have an ocean of power that you're keeping in a fish bowl. Let it go."

"I don't." I stumbled over my words, glaring at the ballerina who nodded at me, agreeing with him. "I don't know how."

"Don't worry, Little Red." He grinned, walking to the window. The phoenix's beak moved, as if whispering something in his ear. He glared at the bird before turning back to me. "We'll teach you how to let loose in no time."

"Oh, you're going to train me, now?"

He shrugged, throwing his legs over the windowsill. "I mean, sure, if that's what you want to call it."

"What would you call it?"

He grinned again, and it was the sort of grin that made my stomach turn. It was the kind of smile that won the hearts of every teenage girl in the world, a smile that broke hearts and inspired dreams. "I call it an adventure."

And just like that, he hopped out of the window.

I gasped and ran toward it, expecting to see a misshapen body crumpled on the ground. I didn't even give it a second thought how he'd gotten up there in the first place. But he was just waiting for me at the bottom, waving. It was too dark to see his face, but his phoenix lit up enough of him to see his smirk. Only his smirk.

When I turned around, the ballerina had her arms crossed over her chest, a flaming eyebrow raised. "What?" I said defensively. "He's cute."

"Hey, I'm not judging," she said as she followed me to bed. "He's better than"—she made a show of shuddering—"Damien. That boy gives me the creeps."

"You're a magical entity," I pointed out. "You're not supposed to get the creeps."

"And you are a woman whose life is at risk. You're not supposed to get feelings for a boy."

"I'm not!" I didn't bother changing clothes as I got into bed. There were more important things to worry about.

"Mmmhmm," she said, nestling into my neck. "I'm just saying, the boy is cute."

I sighed. "He is also dangerous."

"Yes, but what woman in history has ever been able to resist danger?"

CHAPTER 20:

LONG LEASHES

Dinner the next night was absolutely awful. It was truly the most disgusting thing this place had ever put on my plate. Zucchini and eggplant, the two demon-spawn vegetables, on one plate. A true horror.

"This is the first time that I've ever seen you pick at your food like you're Wendy," Patrick noted, jabbing Wendy in the ribs with his elbow. She glared at him.

"This is gross," I complained, my stomach grumbling. "I'd honestly rather eat a week-old mac and cheese."

"To be honest," Nina said, shrugging, "with all the crap they put in the mac and cheese, it would probably still taste exactly the same a week later."

Her joke didn't make me feel any better about my situation. In fact, it only made me hungrier. I would have killed for a plate of mac and cheese right about then. The ballerina hopped on the table to take a sniff of the contents of my plate and made a dramatic gagging gesture. "Do they cook the eggplant in sweaty socks? How do you humans even eat these things?"

"Well," Damien said from beside me, "not everyone can... Wait, what do you live on?"

My familiar rolled her eyes. "Roasted human flesh," she answered sarcastically, using my arm to climb back on my shoulder. "Male flesh, preferably. They crunch the best."

"Okay," said Patrick, pushing his plate away from his body. "That's my appetite gone."

"Agreed," said a voice from behind me—a voice that made my blood turn to ice and then slowly melt as my veins became fire. I turned to find Margot behind me, her face twisted in a cruel smile. "I also lose my appetite whenever I see this one." She flicked my hair, and I could have sworn the room grew silent.

"Maybe you should look at me more often, then," I countered, balling my fists. My knuckles turned white. "You look like you could benefit from skipping a few meals."

"Are you calling me fat?"

"No," I shrugged, turning back around to face the table. "I just think that if you eat less, you'll have less shit to escape from your mouth."

"Excuse me?"

I turned to Wendy. "Don't you find it funny that the mean bitches in school can say whatever they want to whoever they want, but as soon as someone says something back, they get offended? It really gets tiring, Margot. At least when you fling insults around, be prepared to get some back. Trust me, there's a lot about you that people can insult."

"You can't talk to me like that—"

"See, there you go again." I rolled my eyes. "When you start a war, be prepared to finish it the same way. Don't play the victim when the enemy fights back to defend itself."

There was silence, some scraping of plates, and then…

"Lia," Wendy warned, but I was one step ahead.

I grabbed Margot's hand without thinking twice, sensing it above my head. She was holding a plate of food, ready to turn it over and drop it on me. I held her hand in place as I got to my feet and turned to face her. She was taller than me, but in that moment, I felt twice her size. The plate dropped to the floor, breaking on impact.

You could hear a pin drop in the dining hall. No one intervened, and I was grateful for it. This gave me the chance to give her a piece of my mind, to scare her off. I let go of her wrist, looking at her, challenging her. Her nostrils flared.

I didn't think she would stoop so low as physical violence, but I was mistaken. Her hands were circled in sparks, zapping and cracking as she raised her fist. I caught her hand before it could reach my face, and the sparks disappeared when my hand turned to flame. It wasn't hot enough to burn her, to do any permanent damage. I wasn't an idiot. However, there was nothing wrong with scaring her a little. I let the flames eat my entire arm, and then the other. Fire rose like walls around us, trapping us inside. There was no way anyone could get through the flames. No one could get in, and no one could get out.

"Why don't you tell me how weak I am again, Margot?" I let go of her hand and she clutched it, unable to figure out how I was able to absorb her sparks. They weren't nearly as painful as she wanted people to believe they were.

"Let me out of here," she said, her voice a little panicked.

"Tell me, Margot, was that what Erica said when you locked her in that bathroom stall, hmm? Did she beg you to let her out?" She didn't answer, so I stepped forward, raising my voice. "Answer me!"

"Yes," she stuttered.

"And before you pushed Nate into the fountain, did he ask you not to?"

"Yes—"

"Did that stop you?"

"No—"

"Then what makes you think that it will stop me?" I felt powerful, more powerful than I had ever felt in my entire life. "The one person you went out of your way to torment?"

"Help!" she yelled, too scared to touch the flames around her. The idiot. If she had touched it, she would have been perfectly fine. "Can anyone hear me?"

"They can hear you," I assured her, examining my nails. "They just choose not to come to your rescue. Do you know why?"

"Because they're afraid of you?"

I laughed. "No, because they hate you. Everyone in this school hates you, and it's your own fault. This just proves it. People will put their lives and reputation at risk for the people they like. My friends have defended me against you since day one. You know why? Because I am not a complete jerk to everyone I meet."

She started tearing up and I rolled my eyes. "It's a little late for tears, Margot. Any last words?"

"Wait, what? You can't kill me."

"I won't," I clarified. As if reading my mind, the ballerina turned into something else. Something misshapen and twice the size of a normal person. "But she might. See, familiars are very protective of their casters, and you, Margot, have been the single nastiest being in this place. What should stop her from killing you right now?"

"Please, please, I don't want to die."

I stepped closer to her; my mouth was next to her ear now. "Then tell me this… Did you start the fire in the greenhouse? And tell me the truth, Margot. I'll know if you're lying."

"What? No? That wasn't me, I swear. I would never go that far."

I couldn't decide if it was the answer I wanted or not. She was telling the truth, which meant there was a teacher out to get me… Perhaps the very one that accused me in the first place. She seemed like the sort of person who would join the Dark Brotherhood. Yes, she would be the most obvious answer.

I shrugged. "I suppose there's nothing left to do now."

Margot screamed when the creature's maw opened.

She was still screaming when the walls were taken down and the ballerina and I were already back in my seat. Her screaming only stopped when she heard a chorus of laughter.

"Leave me alone from now on, Margot," I said simply, and took a bite of the zucchini.

Gods, I hated zucchini.

CHAPTER 21:

ADVICE FROM AN OLD FOOL

"I don't have the words to tell you how disappointed I am in you." The headmistress paced my room, her heels clickety-clacking with every step she took. It was mind numbing, having to listen to that. I was certain that there was nothing worse than a disappointed parent, but that sound… that was the sound of trouble.

I sat on my bed, watching her as she chewed on a perfectly manicured nail. That was probably a habit I had picked up from her, then. Children adapt to their surroundings very easily. They take on characteristics of the people around them, too. It would have been an interesting observation, had I not been the person on the receiving end of that glare.

As a child, that glare had been what nightmares were made of. There was no way I dared disobeyed her, because I couldn't stand the glare. It spoke louder than anything she could have said or did. I never understood how she managed to do that. It was truly remarkable. I supposed she did have many, many years to practice it on the kids at the academy before I came along. She had a lot of time to master the art of the glare.

I looked over to the ballerina, who was sitting in the window, pretending like she hadn't even been remotely involved in the evening's happenings.

"I don't have to tell you that she was the one who started it," I said, crossing my arms. "She's been tormenting me for years. She's been tormenting all of us for years, but no one has done a single thing about it. Not until now, anyway."

"That doesn't give you a reason to bully her," the headmistress snapped, freezing mid-step to turn to me.

"I wasn't bullying her," I defended myself. "She wanted to empty a plate of food on my head and I stopped her. After that, I asked her a private question, which she answered, and I took down the walls directly after."

Yes, perhaps I was sugarcoating things a little, but I was not afraid to bend the truth slightly. Not where Margot was concerned. I wanted her to suffer the way everyone else in the school has suffered for years. I wasn't going to "do the right thing." Screw the right thing. She had to get a taste of her own medicine for once.

"She said that you summoned a monster to eat her."

I nearly burst out laughing, but I knew that would have gotten me into even more trouble with the headmistress. I found it funny that Margot had gone running to the headmistress as soon as she'd realized everyone was laughing at her, while she called everyone else a snitch whenever they told on her. She was an immature brat. I hated her. I hated people like her so much. It made me wonder what kind of parent would raise a girl like her and let her get away with everything.

I raised an eyebrow at the headmistress, not amused. "I can't stand her, but would I really have her eaten?"

"You wouldn't have her eaten," she agreed in that monotone voice of hers. "But you *would* scare her."

"Exactly. So why am I in trouble and not her?"

"Because I raised you better than this," she said, her voice rising now. "What must everyone think of you, when you go on acting like a child?"

Right, so it wasn't about Margot at all. It was about her image being ruined.

"So, because you raised me," I started, shaking my head. I was so sick of thinking carefully about every word I said, so sick of keeping everything inside. "Because you're worried about what people might think of you, Margot gets to do whatever the hell she wants? I should just take it?"

"I am the headmistress of this school! Her parents are on the committee. They can have me voted out of the academy entirely."

"You're afraid for your job, so Margot can go around terrorizing everyone? And no one can do anything because her parents are on the committee?"

"That's not what I said," she said softly now, sighing.

"But it's what you meant. I've stood by for years, watching her torment the entire school." I got to my feet. "Not a single kid came to help her—not one. Why? Because she's a bitch, and she deserves every nasty thing that comes her way. I hope the next kid gets their chance at her tomorrow, and then the next, and the next. I hope everyone she has ever harmed gets their chance at revenge. I don't care who her parents are. I have more important things on my plate, like people actually trying to kill me. I don't have time to deal with her childish behavior. Her ego is bruised, and that's why she went to you. I didn't summon any monsters, and I definitely didn't send anything to eat her. I told her to stay away from me and I asked her if she was the one behind the fire. That's it."

"I can sense something different in your magic," she said, studying me. "It's wild. I don't like it."

"Of course you don't like it," I huffed, crossing my arms. "You don't like anything that's not fully under control. I was looking for control this entire time, and that was my problem. I've followed your advice and it's nearly cost me my life, multiple times. The burnout was because I was trying to control it. Flames aren't meant to be controlled. They're merely meant to be lit in the right places."

"Does that Abernathy boy have anything to do with this?"

How did I tell her that, yes, Sebastian had everything to do with it? How did I tell her that he was the one who'd made me realize that keeping such a tight hold on the leash on my magic was a bad idea? How did I tell her that everything she had taught me over the years was wrong, that my magic wasn't supposed to be controlled?

Mr. Henry understood. It seemed like he was the only one who did.

How did I tell her that I went against what she told me and decided to trust Sebastian, instead of spying on him like she'd asked? There were things that I just couldn't tell her, not without disappointing and upsetting her. There were few things as bad as disappointing the headmistress, and even though I was in deep crap with her because of Margot, everything concerning Sebastian would have just been the cherry on the cake.

"None of this has anything to do with him," I lied. "He hasn't even been around again."

She saw straight through my lie. "This isn't a game, Cornelia. This isn't some sort of fairy tale. This is your *life* that you're playing with."

"I am not playing with anything," I argued. "It seems like I'm the only one doing anything about the organization that is after my life. It seems like I am the only one doing anything to defend me. The Dark Brotherhood, Margot… Your way hasn't gotten us anywhere. We are still no smarter than we were before we knew about the Dark Brotherhood. There's still no sign of progress. At least I was taking action. If that boy betrays me, I could fight him, and I am pretty sure that I would win. If he betrays me, I wouldn't be angry that I trusted him. I'd rather regret trusting someone than regret not trusting them."

"I can't stop that spitfire heart of yours from making decisions," she said as she walked toward the door. Her face was void of any emotion. That was how I could tell that she was furious. "But heed my warning, Cornelia. It's either going to be your magic or that boy that will kill you, before the Brotherhood even comes close."

"I disagree," I said, looking her straight in the eyes. "I believe that those two things are the only things that will be keeping me alive."

CHAPTER 22:

MIDNIGHT VISIT

There was a different sort of fright that came with being half asleep and being rudely woken up.

When a person was awake, the recovery time was fast, and your brain had the ability to quickly assess the situation. Once your brain had given the all-clear, your body relaxed and that was the end of it.

But when you were half asleep, one foot in your dream and the other half aware of the real world, it took your body much longer to recover. Especially if it was in the dead of night and there was a bounty on your head.

"Wake up," he whispered, shaking me awake. "Hey," he said a little louder.

I startled awake, my heart hammering in my chest. The ballerina rolled off the pillow and crashed to the floor with a soft thump. I looked around the room, scanning it for intruders. I found only one on the bed next to me, a feline grin on his face.

"God, Sebastian," I said, holding a hand over my heart. I could feel it beating and didn't think it had ever beaten so fast.

I glared at him, nostrils flaring. "I should set you on fire right here where you sit. You can't just come in here like this! People want me dead, you know."

"Yeah, sure." He rolled his eyes, getting up and stretching his long arms. "And they're going to wake you before they kill you. Makes sense."

The ballerina floated up to the pillow again, her glare venomous. Oh, she did not appreciate being woken up so rudely. She did not appreciate that at all.

"You are wrong, and I am right," I said, breathing in deeply, trying to get my heart rate down. I knew I was on the brink of a panic attack. That was what happened when a random person shook you awake in the middle of the night. "What is it, Sebastian?"

"You and I are going somewhere."

"Like hell we are," I said, pulling my blanket back over me. The ballerina seemed content with the answer, as well.

He walked back toward the bed, grabbed the end of the blanket, and yanked it off me. "Get up, Little Red. Time's a wastin'."

"I could have been naked under that blanket," I pointed out, tugging at my shorts to make sure they covered everything.

"The first rule about going to boarding school is to never sleep naked or half-naked. You never know when another student will try and prank you," he said before heading over to my wardrobe. His phoenix lit up the contents as he rummaged through it.

"Hey, get away from there!"

He ignored me, picking up items of clothing, pulling a face, and then dropping them. He settled on a pair of jeans and a T-shirt, which he tossed toward me. It landed perfectly on the bed. "Get dressed."

"I am not."

"Listen, Red, I am not taking no for an answer. You either dress yourself or I dress you. Either way, you're coming out with me tonight."

"This sounds a lot like a kidnapping."

"Kidnappings aren't supposed to be enjoyed by the victim. I can assure you that you will be enjoying yourself with me tonight. So, no." He grinned. "It's not a kidnapping."

I gave up arguing with him, then. I could have told him that I was tired, that I wanted sleep more than anything else, but at the same time, there was a feeling of anticipation in my stomach. I was excited to get out of the tower, away from all the drama at the school. I didn't know where he was going to take me, as the nearest town was 30 miles north. Still, despite my exhaustion, despite the events that had occurred earlier that night still haunting me, I quietly grabbed the clothes headed into the bathroom.

Five minutes later, I emerged with brushed teeth and wearing the clothes he had given me. He nodded in approval before tossing me a pair of socks and sneakers.

"You know," I said, pulling on my shoes, "this is the 21st century. Women have the right to choose what they wear."

"Not when they're as stubborn as you. If you had your way, you'd still be in your bed."

"And happily so," I confirmed.

"Stop your whining." He pulled off his hoodie and tossed it toward me. I looked at it in confusion. "You only have bloody blazers. Wear that instead."

I looked at the thin fabric of his long-sleeved T-shirt. It was freezing out. "What about you?"

"I'm hot enough. I don't need it."

This man. This arrogant male.

Perhaps it was a good thing that he was so confident in himself. It seemed like he got stuff done quickly and efficiently. I, on the other hand, had to overthink everything. I had to assess every situation, list my shortcomings, and work around them. Sebastian had the kind of attitude that told me he faced those issues head-on when he encountered them. There was no time to overthink it, in his mind.

I pulled the hoodie over my head without more argument. His scent overwhelmed me: sandalwood and leather, and something… something else. Something musky and a little sweet.

Once he was satisfied with my outfit, he walked to the window and held out his hand toward me. His smile widened. "Come on, Little Red. It's time to take a leap."

"You know, there are stairs."

"Yes, but if you use the stairs, do you get to leap into the unknown? I didn't think so," he answered himself before I could say anything. I bit my lip, contemplating my options. "Do you trust me?"

I realized that I did. I did trust him. Against my better judgment, I trusted him. In fact, I probably trusted him more than anyone else at the academy. Including the headmistress—she'd sooner have me contained than let me run wild. I was free with Sebastian, and I felt confident he would make sure I stayed safe the entire time.

I took his hand and he pulled me close to him. He wrapped his arms around me, then launched us both out of my window.

Before I could scream, we were on the ground and he was grinning like the Cheshire cat. I looked around us, confused as to why we weren't splattered on the dirt.

He sighed. "I'm going to have to give you my secret now, aren't I?" He pointed toward the phoenix. "The familiars are pretty strong."

"He carried us down?" I asked, and Sebastian nodded. I looked over at the ballerina, who was drowsily floating beside me.

"Don't look at me." She shrugged. "I'm not going to do that."

I didn't expect another statement from her, to be perfectly honest. I held the pocket of the hoodie open for her. She was just a little bigger than a Barbie doll, but I was sure she would fit. The sweatshirt reached below my butt, and the sleeves were too long for my arms. The large pocket matched the size of the hoodie.

"I don't know how you are going to fit," I warned, but she was already inside, curling herself up in a tight little ball. I could feel the heat she emitted against my belly. It was comforting.

When I was certain she was secure and only the very ends of her hair escaped the pocket, I turned to Sebastian. "So, where are we going?"

"Hiking."

"Hiking?" I echoed.

"Hiking," he confirmed.

Oh boy.

***

We walked through the forest that I have walked through countless times before. But it was different at night, magical. It was as if someone had taken all the character it had during the day and multiplied it by ten once the sun went down. I could hear the owls hooting. There were a few of them, some big, some small. I could tell by the pitches of their calls. I wished I could see them. I wished I could climb up the trees and pet them. But I very much liked my fingers on my hands and not bitten off, so I kept close to Sebastian instead.

The nocturnal flowers had me gaping. They were brilliantly colored and they shone in the dark. They reminded me of the stars on my ceiling as a child; those stars I used to look at and wish for a normal life. The flowers had me in awe.

"Come on, then," Sebastian called out to me when I fell a little behind. "We're nearly there."

There was a small clearing with a blanket on the grass smack in the middle. A picnic basket sat next to it, and when Sebastian turned to me, I knew that he had set it up beforehand.

"Before you say anything, hear me out. Your room is depressing. The view is great, but as soon as you turn away from the window, I want to stab myself in the eyes. I figured this was a good place to meet up at. You know? Plan and stuff? It's small enough so no one can really find it, and—"

"It's perfect," I interrupted.

"Yeah?" There was a childlike excitement on his face that I wanted to bottle and keep on a shelf, to preserve it forever. It made my heart melt. "You think so?"

"I do."

"Awesome," he said, grabbing my hand and pulling me toward the blanket. "Now, usually I snipe food from the academy's kitchen, but the leftovers looked horrendous, so I had to improvise."

He had me sit down on the blanket before he opened the little basket, revealing the contents inside. There were a few buns, some lunch meat scraps, a few grapes, and a handful of grated cheese in a freezer bag. It was from Cook Magna's personal stash. On cue, my stomach grumbled—the offensive dinner hadn't been nearly enough to satisfy my appetite, and we spent the next half-hour eating.

Looking toward the far side of the clearing, I noticed a rolled-up sleeping bag and a duffel bag. I frowned and looked at him. "You sleep here?"

Sebastien's smile deflated. "Well, yes," he admitted.

"Why?"

"Well, I need to be close to the academy to keep an eye on you. I can't have you being assassinated in your sleep, now can I? We have an adventure to go on. This is the perfect spot. I can watch the stars at night, and I have a perfect view of your tower to see anyone slip in or out of the window. Also, I would see a circus of flames if you had to fight someone off."

"What if it rains?"

He shrugged. "It's been raining most nights this week. I like the rain."

"So do I," I said, popping a grape in my mouth. "But I don't want to sleep in it."

"The trees over there make a good canopy. It stops most of the rain."

It was then that an idea formed in my head. It was a stupid idea, an idea that was going to get me into a lot of trouble if anyone found out about it.

"I have a bathtub..." I began.

He made a face. "Weird flex, but okay."

I chuckled. "No, you idiot. What I meant was that you can sleep in my room, if you want. We can make you a bed in the bathtub and I'm sure it'll be more comfortable than this arrangement."

"You would get into a lot of trouble if you got caught," he pointed out logically.

I nodded. "Yes, but you are very sneaky. You can come in after lights-out and leave again before anyone wakes up. Besides, if someone attacked me, I wouldn't have the chance to defend myself if I'm half asleep. It took me a good few minutes to realize what was going on when you woke me up earlier."

"I'm not going to turn down your offer, Cornelia, but are you sure? I mean, it'll be really hard to resist me when we're in such close quarters."

I whacked his chest with the back of my hand. "Slow down there, Hemsworth."

He chuckled. "Thank you, Cornelia. I will take you up on the offer."

"Lia," I said, as an afterthought.

"What?"

"My friends call me Lia," I explained.

"Well, it's nice to meet you, Lia."

CHAPTER 23:

A LOOK AT THE PAST

"The headmistress thinks that you are out of control." Fiona was floating in the doorway to my bathroom, her arms crossed over her chest.

I rolled my eyes. "It would seem so," I said, stuffing my bag with the books I needed for the day. I didn't need to hear this from Fiona. The headmistress had already told me how she felt, and it was clear that she did not approve of my actions.

"Lia, I want to show you something." She came closer to me and I turned around to face her.

"What is it?"

"I'm going to touch you, and you'll be able to see my past, okay?"

Wait, what? I took a step back, unsure of how to respond.

She moved closer. "You wanted to know what happened to me, right? This is finally the time."

And then she touched my arm, and the world turned to black around me.

***

I was falling down, down, down into a black abyss. The darkness was too black, too thick. It threatened to swallow me up and forget about me. This was the sort of place where things went missing and never emerged again—where dreams came to die, where hope was destroyed, and lives were lost. It was both everything and nothing all at once. It was a cavern, a well, a slide into the unknown, but at the same time; it was emptiness. It was what I imagined nothing would look like if we were able to see it.

And then the blackness shifted, turning into an image covered with inky black spots. Soon, they disappeared, leaving me in a clear classroom filled with students. For a moment, I thought I was back in my own classroom. Did I black out somehow and end up here? I reached out to the person nearest to me, but my hand faded through him. He didn't seven know I was there.

I wasn't in my classroom at all—I was in Fiona's classroom, fifty years ago.

I turned to study the classroom. It still had stone walls like the west wing. Was this before the renovations? It must have been. There were teenagers all over the classroom, littered in groups of two or three. Except for one person.

She was sitting at her desk, a girl with snow-white hair and eyes the color of a night sky. She was beautiful, easily the most beautiful girl in the classroom. There was a crowd huddled around her, cheering as she summoned and vanquished flame after flame, letting it roll over her hands like a tennis ball. Her face lit up whenever someone complimented her fire, telling her that she was the most talented witch at the academy. She was rare, the only one of her kind.

But there was a feeling in her stomach, something that she didn't realize was there until it was too late. I could sense that uncertainty from the other side of the room, and it grew more intense the closer I got to her. I realized I was feeling all of her emotions; I could hear her thoughts as loud as I heard the other kids talking and cheering. She was proud of what she was, but she was also afraid. Afraid of her own power.

"It's all a load of dramatics if you ask me," a boy at the front of the class said, his arms draped over the back of his chair. "What can you do that the rest of us can't?"

She glared at the boy, but there was pain written across her face. She liked him, but it was apparent that he did not feel the same way about her. Every mean comment, every rude whisper to his friends broke her heart a little more each time. I could see the hurt on her face. I could hear the hurt in her mind, feel the hurt in her chest. The boy reminded me a lot of Damien. He was overly confident, but there was something else. Something buried deep within. It was malice, I realized. Hidden far, far below what the eye could see, there was malice. I had noticed it little by little in Damien lately, but I'd thought it was merely the ballerina's warning that was getting to my head. The ballerina…

I tried to find her in the classroom, but she wasn't there. She was still close by, though; I could feel her. She must still be with my physical body.

"Don't listen to him," said a brunette next to the white-haired girl I assumed was Fiona, glaring at the boy. She was short and plump and had flowers braided into her air. I could sense her magic even now. She was an elemental; she was earth. "He's just jealous because he doesn't have a date to the formal yet."

Laura; her name was Laura.

The boy rolled his eyes, turning back around to look in front of him. The excitement died down after he stole it away from the crowd, and Fiona was left alone with the brunette. She turned to her friend. "Why would he be jealous?"

"Because you've gotten at least five offers just now and no one has asked him yet?"

"Then maybe he should ask someone," Fiona huffed, crossing her arms. "It's not my fault I'm actually likeable."

The scene changed then. The colors bled together until another image was formed. We were at the fountain in the courtyard. It had been abandoned for years, but I recognized it immediately. It was beautiful, and the flowers around it made it look like a fairy tale. It was broken down now, overgrown with flora that hid the intricate details in the stones, and was rumored to be haunted. It was rumored to bring nothing but misery and suffering. Not even I dared to get too close. I wasn't superstitious, but something about it made me uneasy.

Fiona sat on the edge of the fountain, reading a book. I couldn't tell what the title was, but I could tell that she was intrigued. She bit her lip as she read, turning the flesh white around her teeth.

"Fiona!" Someone called her name and when she looked up, her face fell. It was the boy from the earlier scene.

"What do you want, Tristan?" she asked, putting her book away and getting to her feet. She wasn't going to stick around to listen to his mean comments.

"You don't have to leave," he said, rubbing the back of his neck. "I just came over to ask if you wanted to go to the formal with me."

Fiona laughed in disbelief. "Excuse me?"

"Do you want to go to the formal with me?" he repeated, and Fiona took a step back, her eyebrows furrowed.

"You're kidding me, right? Why would you ask me? You hate me."

"I don't hate you," he confessed with a shrug. "I actually really like you."

Fiona shook her head. "It doesn't matter. I'm already going with Jeremy."

"Do you really want to go with him?"

Fiona sighed, turning away from him. "Goodbye, Tristan."

"No." He reached out toward her, grabbing her wrist to hold her back. She turned to face him. "Blow Jeremy off. Come with me. I swear I will make it worth your while."

"I'm not like you." Fiona yanked her wrist free of his grasp. "I can't just blow someone off like that."

Tristan sighed. "I'll prove to you that I'm not as bad as you think I am. Come with me. If I prove you right, what did you lose? And if I prove you wrong, well, we'll see where it goes from there."

Fiona considered the offer. I wanted to reach out, to tell her that she shouldn't listen to him. But I couldn't. I was rooted to the spot, forced to watch her make a big mistake.

The scene changed again, and we were in a ballroom. It didn't look like any ballroom I knew. It looked like it was a part of the west wing, but I knew that section of the academy better than anyone. This must have been before the renovations were made. Was the new part of the school really that new?

I couldn't see Fiona anywhere, but then my feet moved, and I realized that I was Fiona. I fought against the movement but couldn't break free. I could feel what she felt, see what she saw, and smell what she smelled. The ballroom was decorated with snowflakes and glitter. It was breathtakingly gorgeous. Music played, tracks I recognized from the 1970s, and the entire ballroom was dancing to the tunes.

Everyone except for Fiona.

Tristan had never bothered to meet her at the fountain like he'd promised, and when she made her way to the ballroom, she saw him... He was dancing with Laura, her best friend. The short brunette laughed as he twirled her around. Fiona's heart dropped to her stomach and she was on the brink of tears. He had convinced her to blow off her date, so he could take another girl. No, not some other girl. Laura—the one person Fiona was certain had her back through thick and thin.

Tristan looked over to her and smiled. My blood went cold. It was the single cruelest expression I had ever seen in my entire life. There was nothing but malice in that smile.

I felt Fiona's blood heat up. It was a feeling I was far too familiar with, one that came with the ecstasy of releasing the magic. It came with finally letting loose and unleashing every flame, every ember that burned in your belly. Fiona's red dress turned into fire, her hair, her eyes, the ends of her limbs. She no longer possessed the power of flames, the flames possessed her. At first, the kids in the ballroom cheered;

Tristan's arrogant face twisted with satisfaction. He had gotten a reaction out of her, the one thing he'd wanted to accomplish by doing this. He had wanted her reaction. He had wanted her to break down and sob.

But she did not fall to her knees, she did not run away. No, Fiona lost every sense of self and gave in to the magic, the wrath. It felt good, it felt so damn good. Her flames started to heat up, no longer offering a pleasantly warm light. No, these flames were much, much hotter and it set the streamers overhead on fire. The cheers of the crowd turned into screams, but she didn't care. She had eyes on one couple only. She didn't know what hurt more, the betrayal of her best friend or the trickery of the boy she had loved for years. Her magic didn't care. Her magic only wanted revenge. It only wanted to be set free.

Without thinking, Fiona wrapped the room in fire, like a present on Christmas morning. Only this present wasn't going to be as fun to open. Because when this present opened, there would be nothing but ash inside.

The doors were cut off by the flames. They were unreachable. I could faintly hear Fiona's name being called, but that didn't distract her. Hands tried to grab her, but the hands of anyone who touched instantly blistered.

The smile faded from Tristan's face, and there were tears running down Laura's cheeks. "We were only dancing," she mumbled, backing away. "He said he was waiting for you, that you were late. Fiona, please calm down."

Fiona didn't care for her excuses. Fiona didn't want excuses; she didn't even want blood. Fiona wanted nothing but ashes.

Laura was the first to burn, her screams louder than those of everyone around her. Tristan wept, begging Fiona. He was begging for his life, apologizing, then begging again. Fiona saw nothing but flames. Fiona *was* nothing but flames, and when Tristan combusted and his cries finally died down, Fiona's mind was her own again.

She turned around, watching as her classmates backed away from her, sweating and pleading for their lives. But she couldn't take back the flames. She couldn't control the fire anymore. Her magic was finally released, and it was hungry — it was hungry for living things.

Fiona's screams matched those of the students her flames devoured. She could hear them even after there was no one else left in the room. She could hear them even when there was nothing but ashes on the floor. The flames licked at the ceiling, broke through the windows. The flames grew closer, closer, closer. They were so close she could touch it. The heat was unbearable.

Fiona screamed one last time as her own flames devoured her, too.

***

I gasped for air, reaching for something; anything.

The pain, the pain was so bad. Tears rolled over my cheeks as I crawled to my bathroom, my insides still burning. They were burning. They were burning. They were burning. I was desperate for any form of release.

I didn't notice that I was screaming until I stopped to breathe.

Everyone in that ballroom… every single one of them died by Fiona's hand. They died because she was stupid and in love. They died because she couldn't control her rage.

She killed them all. She killed them all. She killed them all. She killed them all.

I couldn't get their screams out of my head. It was worse than the pain inside of me. Those cries of agony, of desperation, hoping that someone would hear them, hoping that someone would save them. Every teacher present was killed; no magic could combat the flames. Where was the headmistress? Surely, she could have put out the fire, had she been there? Where was she? Where was she?

"Lia," Fiona's voice echoed in my head and I ignored her, finally reaching the sink where I pulled myself up. The water wasn't cold enough. I needed colder water. I needed to put out this fire inside of me. "Lia," she repeated.

"Get away from me, you psychopath!" I ordered, my nostrils flaring. Fiona retreated. "Why would you show me that? Why would you make me live through that? I felt everything. I felt you die! I felt myself die."

I fell to my knees, burying my face in my hands. She killed them all. She killed them in the same way I would kill everyone if I ever lost control. But I wouldn't… Not like that. Not over a stupid prank.

"Wait, what?" Fiona's voice cracked a little. "Lia, you were only supposed to see snippets, not the whole thing."

"I didn't only see it, Fiona. I lived through it. Why would you show me that?"

"I wanted to show you what giving the flames too much room could do. I wanted to—" Her voice broke. "Lia, oh my God, I am so sorry you had to see that. I didn't… I don't know what happened."

"Get the hell out," I growled. "Go get the headmistress and stay the hell away from me."

"Lia—" Fiona started. I could have sworn that her face had gone paler, but that was impossible. She was a ghost. She was dead. She'd died by fire, just like the rest of her classmates.

Her fire, her anger, her feeling of betrayal. She'd killed them, she'd killed them all. She'd killed herself and burned down the entire building, leaving only the west wing. So many lives were lost that night, and for what? For her revenge? I couldn't stand to look at her. Whether it was because of the look on her face or the disgust that turned my stomach, I didn't know. All I knew was that she had to leave. She had to leave and never come back. I never wanted to see her again. She was no longer my friend.

"Go!" I shouted, tears running more freely now. "I don't want to see you again."

It was the last thing I remembered saying. I passed out before I could watch Fiona disappear into the wall.

CHAPTER 24:

DAMIEN

Nearly two weeks had passed since the incident with Fiona, since I'd passed out on the bathroom floor and the headmistress and Mr. Henry had to lull me back to consciousness with their magic. The headmistress has been fuming ever since. Fiona had somehow trapped me inside of her past's body, and when that body was set on fire, my body thought it was dying, too. My body was reacting to me dying, not to watching someone else die. It reacted as if the flames had consumed me; had burned me to ash.

It took me days to recover. It was worse than a burnout. It was much, much worse than a burnout. I had to sit in bathtubs filled with ice for hours. I watched the ice melt almost instantly around my hot body. The headmistress would drain the bathtub as soon as it heated up again, scared that the water would boil me alive. Sebastien had snuck in every night when I was alone. It was only when he was around that I could sleep. I didn't want to be alone when I dreamed about Fiona's death, when I dreamed about being burned alive by my own flames.

Once I recovered and went back to class again, I felt different, somehow. The ballerina could sense it, too. I had a wariness of my magic that I hadn't had in weeks. The fear was back, and I didn't know how I would ever get rid of it again. The familiar didn't seem to burn as bright anymore, either. My "death" had had an effect on her body, too. We were damaged now, and I didn't know how to put us back together—and neither did the headmistress, although I doubted she even wanted to. She was too happy that I didn't have out-of-control magic anymore. She enjoyed the fact that my flames were weaker and duller now. It meant less for her to worry about.

I still practiced with Mr. Henry, but I was no longer able to keep a flame alive underwater. The flame was dead before it even reached the pool. To my dismay, even Mr. Henry seemed relieved. Were they all so afraid of my magic that, when I was broken and weak, they were happy? They were relieved?

Chewing on the back of my pen, I flipped the page of the tome. I didn't even know what I was supposed to be studying anymore. I found my mind constantly wandering around that fountain, before falling into it and finding nothing but flames at the bottom.

There was a knock at my bedroom door. It was calm and collected, like that hand had knocked on my door a hundred times before. It was Damien.

"Come in," I said, closing the tome. It wasn't going to be read tonight, anyway. I'd been hoping for a distraction for hours. He wasn't the distraction I was hoping for, I realized. But he was a distraction, nonetheless.

Things had been a little weird between Damien and me since the kiss, and I wished it had never happened. Perhaps at another point in time, but not now. Things were too dangerous with me at the moment, and I knew that if we got any closer, Damien would be at risk. Damien would gladly put himself at risk for me, and I couldn't live with myself if anything happened to him. He was the sort of guy that either hated a person with all his might or loved someone with all his heart. There was no halfway with him and right now, it wasn't a good thing. I couldn't protect him in the state I was in; my magic wasn't nearly strong enough to even protect myself.

"Hey, you," he said with a smile as he closed the door behind him. His knuckles were split again, but that was normal for him. He always managed to get into a fight with someone over something. I just hoped this time it wasn't over me. It wouldn't have been the first time. I didn't ask him about it. He would have told me if he'd wanted me to know.

"Hi," I said, matching his smile. "What brings you around?"

"The dorm was getting crowded. Patrick was going on and on about some stupid football game and I just had to get away. I found myself in front of your door."

I nodded. "That sounds like a Patrick thing to do, yes."

He smiled again. There was an awful lot of smiling going on, and I wasn't sure exactly how I felt about it. "Besides," Damien continued, stepping forward, and before I could take a step back, his arms were around my waist, "we haven't had a chance to talk about us."

An uneasiness gripped me. It felt as if my stomach was lined with oil. "Us?"

"Well, yeah," he said, leaning down. Was he going to kiss me again? I swallowed. "I assume that once your secret was out about the ballerina, we would pick up where we left off, but it feels like you've been avoiding me. It feels like everyone gets a chance with you except for me. So I figured it was time I took things into my own hands."

I pushed him away from me before he could lean down any further. He looked at me, shocked. I knew that I'd hurt him by doing that. Why couldn't I just have let him kiss me? Why couldn't I just bring myself to be happy with him? If I only had limited time left, I wanted to spend it with someone I actually enjoyed spending time with. But I couldn't bring myself to do it. If we were in a relationship and something happened to me, it would have killed him. It actually would have killed him. Every day of my life I would worry about what would become of him when I was gone. Perhaps I was overestimating his feelings for me, but if Fiona was right and he really was head over heels, I couldn't do it to him. It was better to shut down whatever this was now than have to do it later and cause more of a fuss.

"There's so much going on, Damien," I said, rubbing my forehead. "I'm sorry. I just don't have the—"

"Screw that, Lia," he exploded. There was a vein bulging in his forehead and his fists clenched. "I have been with you through all the shit in your life. I have stuck by you through every fight, I've stood up for you when everyone was trying to knock you down. This is the thanks I'm getting? You're just going to reject me?"

My mouth went dry. It was as if there was another person standing in front of me. He was no longer my best friend. No, this person was something different. Perhaps this was someone Damien was concealing all of this time.

"What the hell is your problem?" I asked, lava running through my veins. I was taken aback for a moment. Lava… the lava that I hadn't felt since the flashback.

My magic stirred inside of me, a beast waking up from its slumber. It sensed my anger, my distress. It wasn't gone, only dormant. I realized that I had never lost it, but it had stayed away, instead. It had nothing to do with fear, but recovery, instead. If the fire was beneath my skin, I would not have recovered. I needed to cool down first.

It was giving me space. It was protecting me.

"I did the same for you, Damien, and I didn't expect anything back," I retorted, feeling braver. "I didn't expect shit. You're supposed to do all of those things because we're friends, not because you were trying to win me over. And now that I can't be with you, now you throw a damn tantrum?"

"Were," he spat. "We *were* friends."

"That's very mature, Damien." My chest rumbled with magic and I wanted to roar. I wanted to spit the fire that pounded at my chest. "Maybe, if you took the time to listen and tried to understand why I can't be with you instead of acting like a child, we wouldn't be having this conversation. I have too much going on. There's an organization after me, for heaven's sake! They are hunting me down. I can't have you with me when they come for me. I'm doing this to protect you."

"Sure, Lia," he said, his nostrils flaring. "Because I'm just another weakling. Because I need your protection. Don't you remember that I'm always the one protecting you?"

"And now it's my turn," I said, tears stinging my eyes.

"Because no one can be as strong as you? I understand perfectly now. Thank you for explaining that to me."

"That's not what I meant, Damien."

I yelped when he reached over and swept the books from my desk. I looked at him, horrified by his behavior. This was not my friend. This was not the Damien I knew.

From the corner of my eye, I saw the ballerina move closer, blazing brighter than ever. She was ready to protect me when I needed her to. Not just yet. I had to handle this on my own, without magic, first. I had to deal with this in a way where we were on the same level.

I didn't want to bully him with my magic, didn't want to take that chance. If my magic broke through his, which I was sure it was going to do, I could have hurt him very, very badly. I wasn't prepared to witness another death by fire. I couldn't stomach it. Especially not if that person has been by my side for years and years. I couldn't bear even thinking about it. I wondered if he felt the same about him hurting me. I doubted it.

"Get out," I said softly.

"Excuse me?"

The ballerina inched even closer, looking at me, waiting for my command. She was ready to pounce on him and although I knew he deserved to get his ass kicked, I had to give him a chance to get out first. He deserved an opportunity to redeem himself. I owed him that much.

"I said get the hell out, Damien. If you want to act like a child, I don't want to be around you. This is my room, my space, and you are invading it. You are attacking me; you are accusing me of shit that I've never even thought of. You're being a jerk, and I don't want you around when you're being like this—when you're acting like a person that I don't even know anymore. So get out."

Damien opened his mouth to say something but found himself at a loss for words. I was seething, ready to set his hair on fire.

I thought it was over when he walked to the door, but as one last act of defiance, he knocked the sconce clean off the wall. The glass shattered and the flame that was inside got a taste of my carpet, devouring it faster than I could react. What did he think he was doing? Did he think I was going to beg him to help me, to stop the flames?

It was then that I realized he didn't know the extent of my power now. I realized that I had never told him about the progress I was making. It was time to show him. It was time that he understood just how far I had come without his help.

I didn't need his help anymore. I didn't need anyone's help anymore. I had my magic, I had my familiar, and I had Sebastian. The headmistress was no help, and Mr. Henry was acting stranger by the day as my magic grew. I hadn't noticed it at first, not until he was back to normal when my magic was weaker again. But it didn't matter. I didn't need them. I didn't need any of them.

As if reading my mind, the ballerina flew into the fire, absorbing it. She grew bigger, bigger, until she was the size of a human being. Her dress dripped fire, like the liquid flames of the volcano. Damien took a step back, swallowing.

"I said get out, Damien. And don't bother coming back."

There was a look in his eyes that I had never seen in them before. He turned around and stormed out of my room.

CHAPTER 25:

Unexpected Field Trip

"I don't know about you," the ballerina said, back in her smaller form, "but I never want to be that big again." She rolled her shoulders, holding the dustpan for me to sweep up the remains of my rug. The stones beneath it were burned black. That asshole. Just who did he think he was? Who did he think he was, coming in here and demanding things that I had never promised to him?

"I never want to see that ass again," I added, glaring at the door as if Damien was still there. All the sadness and hurt I felt a moment ago has disappeared, and I was now left with nothing but anger.

How dare he? How dare he come in here and insult me like this. After I was only trying to protect him. After I was only trying to do the one thing he had done for me my entire life. I realized then how stupid I had been all this time. I wasn't supposed to avoid him. I had no reason to avoid him, but I was afraid of hurting his feelings. I was afraid of ruining our friendship.

He didn't have that same fear when it came to me. He didn't have that same fear when it came to my feelings, to our friendship. He was out for himself and himself alone. Perhaps, all those times he'd stood up for me, defended me, was done with a hidden agenda. Perhaps he'd wanted me to feel obligated to him, to give him whatever he wanted. He was my hero, after all. Why wouldn't I want to be with my hero?

He never did it because he cared. He didn't do it because he was a nice guy. No, he had fooled all of us. He had fooled me. He was not a nice guy. He was just a very smart guy who was good at pretending to be something he most definitely was not.

"What the hell happened in here?" Sebastian asked. I hadn't even noticed him slipping in through the window.

"Her boyfriend got mad when she broke up with him," the ballerina teased, and I glared at her. She wasn't helping the situation, and yet she was grinning. Why was she trying to make this harder than it already was?

No, that wasn't what she was trying to do. She was trying to lighten the mood, to see how I would react. By the way she was studying Sebastian, I could tell she wanted to know how he would react over the mention of my so-called boyfriend. The little minx was always up to something. I turned to her before Sebastian even had time to reply, snuffing out her flame before she could even get the satisfaction of hearing a reply from him.

"He was not my boyfriend and I did not break up with him. He wanted something more and I told him I couldn't, not with everything going on," I said as I waved my hands in the air, motioning at everything and nothing at the same time.

"The asshole freaked out and nearly set the whole place on fire."

"Shit," Sebastian breathed, crossing his arms. The bastard didn't even offer to help us clean up.

He just stood there, with that infuriating smug look plastered on his face. But, alas, this was all I could really expect from Sebastian. He'd much rather make a snarky comment than be helpful. At least where small things were concerned. I had no doubt he was reliable in a life or death situation.

Still, it wouldn't have killed him to grab a broom.

"He sounds like the type of guy who used to burn ants with a magnifying glass as a child," he added.

I sighed. Under any normal circumstances, I would have laughed at his joke, but right now I was not in the mood. The sad part was that I could actually see him doing it as a kid, now. He seemed like the sort of child who would drown crickets for sport. There was a sort of twistedness about him that I never saw before, and now... Now, I couldn't believe that I had been so blind all these years. He was willing to give up our friendship because he hadn't gotten what he wanted. I'd just lost my best friend because he was being a jerk. Even if we did manage to make peace in the future, things were never going to be the same again. It just showed me how little he actually cared about our friendship. It didn't really matter to him at all, not if it was this easy for him to walk away from it.

I heard whispering, then looked up to see Aodh's beak moving close to Sebastian's ear. Whatever it said, Sebastian didn't move a muscle in his face. It was as if he wasn't even listening. When he saw me staring at him, he smiled and shrugged nonchalantly. "Seeing as your evening just cleared up." He motioned to the desk and the textbooks that were scattered on the floor. I groaned, I'd forgotten about that. "You and I are going out."

"Sebastian, I really don't feel like —"

"I have news, but I can't tell you here," he offered, pointing at the door. He was right. Talking here was dangerous. Especially since there was a certain ghost who had made it her business to interfere with mine. If she heard something interesting, I had no doubt that she would take it to the headmistress, and they would want to step in and stop us.

They wouldn't like any plan we managed to come up with, and although they had no power over us — nothing nearly strong enough to keep Sebastian and me from doing whatever we wanted — I chose not to get violent at all. Tonight was enough violence for me with people that I held dear to my heart. I didn't want to go through what I had experienced tonight with anyone else I loved. Especially not the headmistress. She was the only family I had. I didn't think I could stomach even thinking about harming her. No, we had to play it safe. We had to stay as quiet as possible and we had to steer clear of anything that might prove an obstacle for us. The less any of them knew about what we were planning or doing, the better. They wouldn't understand, anyway.

"Now will you please put down the broom and come with me?"

"Fine," I said, getting up to set the broom by the door before grabbing Sebastian's hoodie. "But this had better be good."

"Your good or my good?" he asked with a grin. I fought the urge to set his hair on fire.

"Good is good," I said as I pulled the hoodie over my head.

He nodded, curling his bottom lip as if he was impressed with my answer. "Fair point."

***

It didn't take us very long to reach the clearing where we met up every night. Sure, he slept in my room, but privacy was an issue. Even if they knew he was in my room, the headmistress wasn't above letting me think that I was getting away with it, only to let Fiona spy on our conversations.

No, we continued to meet up in the clearing—we spent as much time there as we possibly could, then made our way back to my room in the morning hours when we decided it was time to sleep. I had asked Sebastian to help me with my magic, but after the incident with Fiona, I was too embarrassed to even show him what my magic had become. I refused every night he offered, claiming that it was too dangerous. He didn't mention the fact that I was the one who'd asked him to help me in the first place, but it was a hole in my lie that we both chose to ignore.

He knew that I was struggling, and he didn't push me or call me out. I appreciated that. What he said next, though, I didn't appreciate so much.

"They're coming."

"Wait, what?" I asked, turning around to face him. He was rubbing the back of his neck. "I thought we had at least another month. You said—"

"I know what I said," he snapped, pushing a hand through

his hair. He rubbed his hands together, then pushed them into his front pockets. As if deciding that it wasn't comfortable for him, he moved them to his back pockets. They were at his sides a moment later. I had never seen him so anxious, so restless. It made me uneasy. I hated it. He was the calm one, the collected one. He was the anchor in this relationship, and I was the rocking boat on the ocean. "Things must have changed while I was away."

It was my turn to push my hand through my hair, the ballerina scowling at me when I accidently knocked her with my hand. I cringed an apology before addressing Sebastian again. "How do you know they're coming?"

"I can feel it," he said, looking up at the sky as if he could see something that I couldn't. "I grew up with that tainted magic around me. I know how to sense it. I know what to look for."

I chewed on my thumbnail. I didn't even know that I was pacing until I stopped to look at him. "How long do we have?"

The look on his face told me a million truths, then—truths that I didn't want to hear. His face flashed with sorrow, with pain and anger all at once. I wanted to hug him and hit him. I wanted to kiss him.

No, not now.

"They're already here, aren't they?" I asked, my voice so soft, I didn't even think he was able to hear me. I couldn't say it any louder, as if that would make it a reality. Perhaps, if I didn't speak about it at all, it wouldn't be real; it wouldn't happen. It was stupid, I knew. But I was desperate.

"Yes," he admitted guiltily. "I just had to get you out. We can't fight them. Not like this. Your power is still mostly dormant, and I don't have enough magic on my own to take them on."

He looked at me, then at the familiar and back at me again. As if he sensed something that he didn't before. "Your magic, it's back to the way it was before," he said, and he didn't seem excited about it. "Even with it being back, we can't fight. We honestly don't stand a chance. Not with our current pools of magic. We needed the time to dig deeper, to explore more. Everything happened too fast and we didn't have time to prepare. I should have known this was going to happen. We need to leave." He went to grab my arm, but I pulled away.

"But the academy…"

"The academy has defenses in place," Sebastian said. "Once they realize that you aren't there, they will leave. They have no business with the lesser sorcerers."

"My friends are there, Sebastian!" I turned to run back to the academy but was caught in his hands.

"You're not going back there until they've left." His voice was final, stern. It was the voice I wouldn't normally have fought against, but this was different.

"Sebastian," I raged, kicking the air. "They're going to die."

"If you go there, *you* are going to die."

"It's a sacrifice I'm willing to make," I said, meaning every single word. I was happy sacrificing myself for them, for my friends and for the only family I had.

"But it's not one I am willing to make." His words hit me like a brick, and I stilled in his arms, letting it sink in. "And it's not only because I need your help. Which is part of the reason, I must admit, but it's not the whole reason." He turned me around to face him. "Somehow, in these last couple of weeks, you've wormed your way into my heart and I can't seem to get you out.

"I've spent my whole life thinking that I was the only one of my kind. My father groomed me to be a weapon, to take over the Brotherhood one day, and I was alone for most of my life. But then I heard about another elemental that my father was keeping an eye on. He'd been watching you for years, assessing your powers once every month," Sebastian explained.

"Your magic just seemed to get stronger and stronger, and when I overheard him talking about you, about this great witch that had magic that could rival mine, I had to get to you. For so long, it has been my only mission in life. And then I found you, this beautiful woman with hair like fire and now I can't see how to let go of you. I have this connection to you, and I know it's weird, but it just feels like we are meant to be together. If not in a romantic sense, then in friendship. Although, I wouldn't complain about the former."

That was when I reached up, stood on my tiptoes, and kissed him.

I couldn't tell you why I did it. I hadn't noticed any feelings developing for him before that night. We were friends, friends who'd known each other for a very short period of time. But he was right. We had a connection.

Everything about us being together felt right, and when our lips touched, there was fire around us. Our flames met, dancing, combining, teasing. It was as if I had found the missing piece to the puzzle that I didn't even know I was building. It was the piece of the puzzle that I'd needed all this time—all this time that I felt like I didn't belong, like I just wanted to be normal. With Sebastian, I *was* normal. With Sebastian I wasn't a freak; I was the same as him. I was too powerful for my own good.

His lips were soft against mine and he tasted like mint. He wrapped his arms around me, pulling me closer into him. He held me tightly, as if I would disappear at any second.

"You piece of shit liar!"

"You piece of shit liar!"

I pulled away from Sebastien as soon as I heard Damien's voice echo through the clearing. My blood went cold and I turned around. Damien was storming toward us. I kept Sebastien behind me despite his best efforts to get in front of me to protect me from this maniac.

"You gave me some bullshit excuse about not being ready for a relationship, and then you go off with this guy? Who even is he, huh?"

"I'm the guy who's going to kick your ass if you don't cool the hell down," Sebastian said, his chest rumbling with rage. I felt the fire behind me, felt the lava that was running through his veins. I could feel it in the same way I felt my own. The scent of his fire hung in the air, and then I sensed it, that crippling aura that he'd revealed the first time we met. It didn't hit as hard this time, but I could feel it around me. It was comforting and warm, just like his flames. Damien didn't seem to notice. Of course he wouldn't have. He was immune.

"Stay out of this, Abercrombie," Damien hissed, his eyes not leaving my face. The ballerina and phoenix were beside me now, ready to attack at my command. Damien's face was contorted in anger. He didn't seem hurt... no, this was rage. This was pure and utter rage.

"I told you I didn't have a good feeling about him," the ballerina whispered. "He's obviously crazy."

"Hey, man, she doesn't owe you anything," Sebastian said, his hands on my shoulders. His head stuck out completely above my own. I didn't realize exactly how tall he was until that moment.

Damien's footsteps didn't slow as he got closer, and closer, and closer. It didn't seem like he was ever going to stop.

"Damien," I said softly, tears stinging my eyes.

"I followed the trail of your magic," he said, shaking his head. "I came to apologize."

"I—"

"But it seems like there is no need for me to apologize, now is there?"

Anger burned the back of my throat. "Of course, you have to apologize!" I said, stepping forward. "You acted like a madman, and now what? What are you going to do?" I watched his fists clench. "Are you going to hit me? I did nothing wrong. I don't owe you anything, Damien. I was telling the truth when I told you all those things."

As if my words had triggered him, he pulled back his hand. I closed my eyes, waiting for the blow. Never in my life had I imagined that Damien would hurt me. Never had I thought that he had a single malicious bone in his body. But the ballerina had known, and she had warned me. I hadn't listened, and now I was going to get punched in the face by my best friend—who might just have been a complete psychopath from the beginning.

The blow never came and when I opened my eyes, Damien's fist was caught in midair by Sebastian's.

I was yanked out of the way. I couldn't tell if Sebastian pushed me or if the familiars were to blame. But I watched in horror as the two men went head to head, fists flying.

I only realized after a moment why Sebastian wasn't using his fire. It was useless against Damien. His magic, though underrated, was pretty powerful. Many people underestimated him because he didn't have a physical power, but I always knew that, in a different way, Damien was more powerful than all other witches combined.

Having the power to nullify any and all magic? Sometimes I wonder if Damien isn't unfairly overpowered. He doesn't have a burnout point, not like the rest of us. His magic is infinite.

Sebastian had to rely on brute force and in this case, I was certain he had the upper hand. He landed punch after punch, but every now and then he grunted as Damien sucker-punched him.

Damien fought dirty. I should have known he'd fight dirty. He was never one to play a fair game. He always wanted to show off, to beat another person. He didn't care how he did it, so long as he won.

I tried to step in, but the familiars held on tightly to each arm. I couldn't move. All I could do was watch in horror as the two boys fought because of me. My stomach twisted with guilt, even though I knew that Damien was being unreasonable.

An explosion came unexpectedly from the academy, and another wave of guilt crashed over me. They were here because of me. They were here, looking for me, and everyone at the academy was going to pay for it. Damien took advantage of the distraction and hit Sebastian square in the chin, and Sebastian stumbled backwards, clutching his jaw.

His eyes lit up with fury as he pointed a finger to Damien. "You're dead," he mumbled.

I caught the familiars off-guard when I broke free of their hold on me. Anger took over my body, and I was only half aware of what I was doing.

I leapt onto Damien, screeching like a banshee.

I attacked him, assaulted him with every weapon on my body. I punched him, slapped him, scratched a line down his face that would certainly scar. I was like a feral animal. Strong hands grabbed me around the waist and lifted me off Damien, but I fought against the grip and when he set me down, I was ready to leap again. I turned around to show Damien my wrath when Sebastian hit him one more time and my best friend fell to the floor, out cold.

I found it funny, in a way. He had crumpled to the floor just like our friendship had.

CHAPTER 26:

WHAT HAPPENED HERE?

The academy was in shambles, debris and bodies everywhere. Some were still breathing, but to my horror, some were not. I never thought that it would come to this.

I knew that they were going to come for me, and I knew they wouldn't take pity on anyone who helped me. But these were kids, teenagers. *I* was still a teenager. Sebastian was nineteen; he was still a boy. He was still so young, and he had to go through all of this. And something told me that this was not the first massacre he had been forced to see. I hoped with every bone in my body that this would be my last, even though I knew there was still a war to come. This was only the first battle.

The main structure of the academy still stood, but pieces of brick and stone had been blasted from the walls and had crushed some students and teachers. Still, that wasn't as bad as what was around them—at least I couldn't see the faces of the crushed victims, I couldn't see the horror on their faces as they had breathed their last breath. Those faces were going to haunt me for years and years to come. That was, of course, If I lived long enough.

The bodies of the dead that weren't crushed were still mangled. Some were torn up, others had holes right through their chests. Some seemed to have no blood left in their bodies at all. They looked deflated, drained—as if someone had sucked the life right out of them. I wanted to cry, to scream, to mourn the dead, but I couldn't. I couldn't bring myself to cry. Perhaps I was in shock. No, I was pretty sure that I was in shock. Everything felt too surreal to me, like I was watching a horrible movie. Imagining that it wasn't happening was better than accepting the reality of what was actually going on. It was better than knowing it was my fault these people were dead. It was my fault that they'd died without even knowing why. They didn't even know who the Dark Brotherhood was. That was the saddest part of it all.

"Cornelia." I heard my name being breathed as a prayer and, before I knew it, I was wrapped in warm arms. I couldn't help the tears that fell as the headmistress hugged me, holding on to me for dear life.

Finally, some tears. But it still didn't feel real. I didn't have the usual tightness in my throat or the burning eyes. It was as if my eyes were merely leaking. I would have been glad about it, had I not known that I was going to feel the full extent of guilt and sadness later, when I had time to process everything. When I had time to think about what had caused this and how, exactly, each of them had died.

What was the last thing I said to them? Have I ever even spoken to them?

"I thought I had lost you," the headmistress said. "I thought they took you. Oh, my sweet, sweet girl."

"It's okay," I managed between sobs. "I'm okay."

It was, in fact, *not* okay. Not in the slightest, but I knew that if I told the headmistress what was really going on in my head, she would have scolded me, told me that I shouldn't linger on things that I could do nothing about. She would have told me that I was being silly for making a fuss. That this was supposed to happen, to start a new chapter in my life. I knew what she was going to say, and I didn't need to hear it again. Because no matter how much she said it, it wouldn't have changed the way I felt at that moment—like a villain. A coward.

"How?" she asked, holding me at arm's length. It was only then that she noticed Sebastian standing behind me.

For a moment, I thought she was going to attack him. I expected her to toss me to the side and wring his neck, but she didn't. Somehow, she knew that he was the reason I wasn't in direct danger. Somehow, in that weird way of hers, she knew that he was the one who had gotten me out, who would have protected me with his life, if it had come to that.

It must have been nice knowing nearly everything.

"You kept her safe?" she asked him, her voice breaking.

"I think she is more than capable of keeping herself safe," he replied nonchalantly, pushing his hands into his pockets. I could have sworn his cheeks were turning a little red, though it was impossible to tell in the dim lighting of the moon that shone through the holes of the walls and ceiling. "I just got her away in time."

To my surprise, the headmistress reached out and hugged him. He seemed awkward, as if he didn't know what to do. I could tell that he wasn't used to it, to hugging and thankfulness. To anyone showing gratitude for something he did. Everything was expected of him and when he did it, he was just doing his job. He received no praise for it, no reward. But now, he got to experience it from one of the greatest witches in history.

Gingerly, he wrapped his arms around her, too.

"Thank you," she said, repeating her words over and over. "I can never thank you enough."

When she was done, she let go of Sebastian—who looked a little taken aback—and straightened her skirts. It was time for her to be the headmistress again. The time for playing the doting mother has passed, and she was back to her stoic self in no time. I couldn't decide which version of her I preferred.

She looked around at the bodies on the ground, at the nurses who tended to the wounded. "They came out of nowhere," she started, relaying the events of the evening to us. "They spared no one. The ones that are still breathing are only lucky. I killed four of them in my office, another four in your bedroom. They had someone on the inside."

"Mrs. Finnick," I mumbled, cursing the name. "It wouldn't surprise me. That woman is wretched."

"No," the headmistress said. "It was Mr. Henry."

"What?" My whole world seemed to disappear from beneath my feet. Mr. Henry, the person I had trusted the most. The one who had helped me. The one who knew about things that he wasn't supposed to know about, and the one who had unlimited access to information straight from the source: me. He knew every extent of my magic, every weakness, every hole.

"He knew that my magic was dormant," I said, more to myself than anyone else. "He knew that I was weak, that I wouldn't have been able to fight back. That was why he came tonight. That was why he came for me tonight."

"He led the troops." The headmistress seemed to scold herself in her head. It was entertaining to imagine her giving herself a lecture—one of those lectures that I have endured many, many times. I would have enjoyed it, if it hadn't been for the circumstances. "I think he was the one who started the fire, too, in an attempt to alienate you from the rest of the school. If no one wanted anything to do with you, you were easier to take without anyone knowing. But when you weren't in your tower…"

"They went looking elsewhere," I mumbled. The headmistress nodded. It made perfect sense. Sebastian had said there was possibly someone on the inside. If he'd started the fire, he would have gotten me suspended, alienated. But he had defended me… Unless it was because he wanted me to trust him, to confide in him. He'd defended me so I was obligated to trust him. Damien and Mr. Henry could have been the same person.

"Nina, Wendy, and Patrick," I said, wiping the tears from my face as I suddenly remembered my friends. "Are they okay?"

The headmistress shrugged. "I don't know, dear. I only came down from your tower now. I haven't had the chance to assess the damage or casualties yet."

I scanned the room, finding Wendy furiously digging. My heart sank and I ran toward her. Sebastian was close behind me.

"Wendy?" I asked, gingerly touching her shoulder. She looked up at me with teary eyes. It was strange seeing her without makeup. I supposed I never really saw her after dinner.

"Patrick," she mumbled. Her nails were starting to bleed. I looked over at Sebastian, whose face paled. He knew what the state of his body would be in if Patrick was under the massive boulder.

I crouched down beside my friend, holding her as she sobbed. Wendy was the tough one, the one who didn't take crap from anyone. She was the aloof one, the scary one. I never thought I would see her in this state.

A hand peeked through the stones, a silver ring on its middle finger—a ring etched with the tree of life. Patrick's ring. I pulled Wendy closer to me, holding her as tight as I possibly could. I didn't know whether it was because I needed to hold someone, or because she needed someone to hold her, but I held. I held for dear life. I held until her shaking had stopped and her sobs had turned into small whimpers.

"They're not going to stop," Sebastian said, his hand on my shoulder. I leaned my head to the side to touch his hand with my cheek.

"I know. We have to stop them before this happens to anyone else."

"Lia!" Nina's voice rang out and I could have cried with relief. She ignored Sebastian entirely, pulling Wendy and myself into a tight bear hug.

I saw Sebastian slip off out of the corner of my eye, leaving us to grieve the loss of our friend in peace. I didn't know if Damien was coming back, but I chose not to tell the girls about that just yet. They had enough to deal with for one night.

But tomorrow, tomorrow I would tell them everything, and then I would make a plan. This could not happen again. I refused. I couldn't let it. This was bigger than I had initially thought. If the Brotherhood went to this extreme to get one girl, I didn't want to know what they would do to get a world. Millions of lives would be lost, and they wouldn't care.

Tonight, I would grieve. I would grieve the loss of Patrick and my best friend. I would grieve the loss of my favorite teacher, and I would grieve the loss of everything in between. And then tomorrow, I intended to wake up with the new dawn, to find a way to take down the Dark Brotherhood, the corrupt council, and every other traitor to our kind.

There will be no more lives lost for this idiotic cause. I would make sure of that. Even if it was the last thing I did.

EPILOGUE

There was a horrible smell in the air. It reminded Damien of sewer water in the city. He had been to enough rough neighborhoods to know what that smelled like. Actually, he'd *lived* in enough rough neighborhoods. The smell reminded him of home, of his childhood. He hated it.

He could sense the magic, feel it in his bones. There was a wrongness to it, the sort of wrongness that made up everything evil in the world. The sort of wrongness that was only read about in books. It made his heart beat faster. It didn't have the sweet, innocent smell of the magic he was used to. Gods no, this was completely different. He wasn't even sure if he could call it magic to begin with. It was power, not magic, and this power was something a lot of people longed to have. Damien understood how people could get addicted to this much power. He could understand how this could become a lifelong obsession. Yes, he understood—and he wanted in.

He stood in the man's office. The fire crackled in the fireplace, sending long shadows across the hardwood floor. The room was decorated with leather and wood, a few furry pelts strewn across the sofas and floor. Damien took in every inch of his surroundings, marking the exits in his head. If he had to bolt, if he had to run, he needed to know exactly which route to take. Damien was certain he could outrun any grown man, but he wasn't going to take any chances. This magic was unpredictable. For all he knew, this power could have turned the casters into superhumans.

"You're telling me that my son has been feeding information to the academy?" the man asked, his voice rough. Damien saw the resemblance between himself and his son.

The striking blue eyes and pitch-black hair, the slight accent, the resting face of arrogance. Yes, they were definitely related, but where the man's son was nothing but wildness and rebellion, this man was collected and calm. His face didn't show a sliver of emotion, and it unsettled Damien. Had this power stripped it all down? Had this power taken away his ability to feel?

He hoped so. He hoped that he would one day taste it for himself.

When the men had found him in the clearing, he had been certain that he was going to die. Those men weren't the sort to take any captives. But those men weren't men at all, they were misshapen and mutated. They were ugly and brutish, with teeth that could tear skin from bone as easily as a wolf.

"Yes, sir," Damien confirmed, nodding as if his words alone were not enough.

They'd asked him where the boy was, the one named Sebastian. They'd tracked his magic to the clearing, but the trail had gone cold from there. Damien assumed it was the boy who was kissing Lia, *his* Lia. The one he had protected and loved since they were children. The one who he had stood up for, every single time. The one that had betrayed him and tore his heart from his chest. He felt hollow now, as if he were only a husk of a human being. A husk filled with only one thing: revenge.

He told the men what had happened and where they might have gone. When they turned to leave him, he'd begged them, actually begged them, to take him with them. If they were looking for the boy, if they were chasing him, they wanted him dead. It just so happened that he also wanted the boy dead.

He wanted that guy dead more than he had initially realized. He'd thought he hated the guy when he'd kissed Lia, but when he'd humiliated Damien in front of her? That was when he had started to really detest the guy. And when Lia had done nothing but stand there and watch, when she had attacked Damien like that, she'd made it on his list, as well. How dare she? After everything he had done for her, after all the battles he had fought for her.

Yes, Damien was hurt, but he was also insulted. Lia wasn't the girl he thought she was, and she'd tricked him into protecting her, into liking her. She had used him and he'd had enough of it. Now, he would do everything in his power to bring those two down. Even if it meant siding with this wretched smell and the people it followed.

The man sighed, sitting up in his leather chair. His desk was neat, as if no one even worked there. Damien knew better than to trust anyone with a tidy desk. His own father had always kept his desk neat, but he was the biggest scum of all. Damien's mother would agree. Or, well, she would if she had the guts to. Perhaps she would have if his father wasn't around with a waiting fist. No, he didn't think she had it in her. It had been beaten out of her years ago.

"And you decided to come willingly with my guards, why? What do you want, boy?"

"The fire witch," Damien said, spitting the very mention of her. "She isn't who I thought she was. I no longer have faith in her cause like I used to. I wish to switch sides. It also helps that your son was the one who seduced her. I want to make him pay as much as I want to see her magic drained from her body."

The man nodded, rubbing his chin. "People often disappoint us in the cruelest ways. But I cannot invite you to join the Brotherhood merely because she broke your heart. Oh, don't look so surprised—I know a broken heart when I see it."

Was it a broken heart that he had? Damien wouldn't have known, even if it hit him in the face. He'd only ever loved one girl and she hadn't broken his heart until now. He knew what hatred felt like, though, and this was definitely a part of it. But he didn't argue with the man. He had a feeling that the man didn't take kindly to anyone who went against his word.

"I can offer you information," Damien said instead. "I have been friends with the fire witch for years. I know how she thinks, I know what her weaknesses and strengths are. I have also basically grown up in the academy. I know every tunnel, every weak spot."

"I already have inside information," the man said, pointing to the figure standing in the corner. Damien hadn't noticed it until now. It was as if the figure had appeared out of thin air. It must have, as Damien had scanned every inch of the office as soon as he entered. There had been no other people in there, other than the man behind the desk. Another effect of the power in this place, perhaps? It wouldn't have surprised Damien. He had come to believe in the impossible when it came to magic. Especially after Lia had gotten her talking familiar. Even the impossible was possible with the right sort of magic and manipulation. No one could say there was anything that was impossible anymore.

Damien wasn't surprised at who he saw in the shadows. He always knew the man was a snake.

Mr. Henry stepped forward, a sly grin on his face. It was sleazy and dark, and it unsettled Damien. It wasn't the smile that everyone at the school loved. He had tricked all of them, every last one. Damien smiled back at him, refusing to let his uneasiness show. He didn't doubt this power had the ability to sense it, but he had to pretend like it wasn't bothering him. Even if only for his own sanity.

"Cornelia considered you her closest friend," Mr. Henry purred, his footsteps even and heavy. "She really must have pulled a number on you. Was it the boy she's been with?"

"You knew?" the other man said, his eyes accusatory. Mr. Henry threw his hands up.

"Hey, I only told you what you wanted to know. You never asked if she had help, so it wasn't my place to say anything." Mr. Henry paused, looking at Damien once again. "It seems the secret has brought a new partner our way. You are very welcome, Olaf."

He winked at the man in the chair. Something told Damien that no one else would have gotten away with it—not without losing an eye in the process.

The man shrugged, shifting his attention back to Damien. "I suppose you're right, Adam. Still, I do not see how you could be of any more use to us than Adam already was."

Damien shrugged. "Like I said, I know the academy better than anyone. There's a difference between a teacher who could go wherever he wanted whenever he wanted, but us students have to sneak around. We have to get out somehow. I know every hidden entrance and exit—something our good professor over here clearly doesn't know about. If he had, there wouldn't have been as many casualties on your side as there were."

"The kid's got a point," Mr. Henry—no, Adam—said. "There's also the matter of his magic that we need to discuss. It can be of great use to us."

"My magic?" Damien's interest was piqued. No one had ever taken any interest in his magic, not really. Not unless they wanted to study it to see how it worked. Other than that, people were merely afraid of him and his magic.

Adam nodded. "I have been working on a project. It's a small one, still in progress as we speak, but I have been missing one ingredient. I think that ingredient might be in your magic."

Olaf smacked his hands together, grinning. "It seems we might have lost the battle, but the war is still up for grabs. Welcome to the team, kid."

After a brief handshake, he called in one of his guards. "Find my son," he said, venom lacing his words. "Keep an eye on him until I give the word. Do not engage—and if he is hostile, don't kill him. I want to do that myself."

To Be Continued...

BONUS!

Want a FREE Paige Stonebank short story Ebook based on the 'Enchanter Witch Academy' World?

GO TO THIS LINK FOR YOUR FREE 'ENCHANTER WITCH ACADEMY' EBOOK!

bit.ly/enchanterwitchacademy

Lastly…

If you enjoyed this book, then I'd like to ask you for a favor. Would you be kind enough to leave a review for this book on Amazon? It'd be greatly appreciated!

See you in 'Enchanter Witch Academy' Book 2.

Thank you for reading,

Paige Stonebank